'I want you back in my life, my home and in my bed.'

He declared this with a deep, dark, husky ferocity. 'I don't want us to fight or keep hurting each other. I want us to be how we used to be before life got in the way. I want it all back. Every sweet, tight, glorious sensation that tells me you are my woman. And I want to hear you say that you feel the same way about me.'

With her body crushed to the wonderful hardness of his body, and their eyes so close it was impossible not to see that he meant every passionate word, offering him anything but the truth seemed utterly futile.

'Yes,' she whispered. 'I want the same.'

Michelle Reid grew up on the southern edges of Manchester, the youngest in a family of five lively children. But now she lives in the beautiful county of Cheshire with her busy executive husband and has two grown-up daughters. She loves reading, the ballet, and playing tennis when she gets the chance. She hates cooking and cleaning, and despises ironing! Sleep she can do without, and produces some of her best written work during the early hours of the morning.

Recent titles by the same author:

THE SHEIKH'S CHOSEN WIFE
ETHAN'S TEMPTRESS BRIDE
THE ARABIAN LOVE-CHILD

A PASSIONATE MARRIAGE

BY
MICHELLE REID

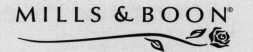

MILLS & BOON®

First published in Great Britain 2002
Harlequin Mills & Boon Limited,
Eton House, 18-24 Paradise Road, Richmond, Surrey TW9 1SR

© Michelle Reid 2002

ISBN 0 263 83205 8

Set in Times Roman 10½ on 12 pt.
01-0203-53654

Printed and bound in Spain
by Litografia Rosés, S.A., Barcelona

CHAPTER ONE

LEANDROS PETRONADES sat lazing on a sunbed on the deck of his yacht and looked out on the bay of San Estéban. Satisfaction toyed with his senses. The new Spanish resort had developed into something special and having enjoyed a very much hands-on experience during its development, he felt that sense of satisfaction was well deserved. Plus the fact that he had multiplied his original investment, he was business-orientated enough to add.

He had done a lot of that during the four years since he took over from his late father, he mused idly. Multiplying original investments had become an expectation for him.

Which was probably why he'd found this project just that bit different. It had always been more than just another investment. He had been in on it from the beginning when it had been only an idea in an old friend's head. Between them, he and Felipe Vazquez had carefully nurtured that idea until it had grown into the fashionable new resort he was seeing today.

The problem for him now was, where did he go from here? The resort was finished. The luxury villas dotted about the hillside had their new owners, the five-star hotel, golf and leisure complex was functioning like a dream. And San Estéban itself was positively bustling, its harbour basin filled with luxury sail crafts owned by the rich and famous looking for new places to hide out while they played. By next week even this yacht, which had been his home while he had been based here, would have slipped her moorings. She would sail to the Caribbean to await the arrival of his brother Nikos, who planned to fly out with his new bride in three weeks.

It was time for him to move on, though he did not know what it was he wanted to move on to. Did he go back to Athens and lose himself in the old cut and thrust of the corporate jungle? His wide shoulders shifted against the sun bed's padded white cushion as an old restlessness began to stir deep within his bones.

'No, it is not possible to go over the top with this.' A soft female voice filtered through the open doors behind him. 'It is to be a celebration of San Estéban's rebirth, and a thanks and farewell to all who worked so hard to make the project happen. Let it be one of fireworks and merriment. We will call it—the Baptism of San Estéban, and it will become its annual day of carnival.'

A smile eased itself across his mouth as Leandros listened, and his shoulders relaxed as the restlessness drained away. The Baptism of San Estéban, he mused. He liked it.

He liked Diantha. He liked having her around because she was so calm and quiet and so terribly efficient. When he asked her to do something for him she did it without bothering him with the irritating details. She was good for him. She tuned in so perfectly to the way of his thinking.

He was almost sure that he was going to marry her.

He did not love her—he did not believe in love any more. But Diantha was beautiful, intelligent, exceedingly pleasant company, and she promised to be a good lover—though he had not got around to trying her out. She was also Greek, independently wealthy and was not too demanding of his time.

A busy man like him had to take these things into consideration when choosing a wife, he pondered complacently. For he must be allowed the freedom to do what was necessary to keep himself and the Petronades Group of companies streets ahead of their nearest rivals. Coming from a similar background to his own, Diantha Christophoros understood and accepted this. She would not nag and complain and make him feel guilty for working long hours, nor would she expect him to be at her beck and call every minute of the day.

She was, in other words, the perfect choice of wife for a man like him.

There was only one small obstacle. He already had a wife. Before he could begin to approach Diantha with murmurings of romance and marriage he must, in all honour, cut legal ties to his current spouse. Though the fact that they had not so much as laid eyes on each other in three years meant he did not envisage a quick divorce from Isobel being a problem.

Isobel…

'Damn,' he cursed softly as the restlessness returned with enough itchy tension to launch him to his feet. He should not have allowed himself to think her name. It never failed to make him uptight. As time had gone by, he had thought less and less of her and become a better person for it. But sometimes her name could still catch him out and sink its barbed teeth into him.

Going over to the refrigerated drinks trolley, he selected a can of beer, snapped the tab and went to rest his lean hips against the yacht rail, his dark eyes frowning at the view that had only made him smile minutes before.

That witch, the hellion, he thought grimly. She had left her mark on him and it still had not faded three years on.

He took a gulp of his beer. Behind him he could still hear Diantha's level tones as she planned San Estéban's celebration day with her usual efficiency. If he turned his head he would see her standing in his main stateroom, looking as if she belonged there with her dark hair and eyes and olive-toned skin, her elegant clothes chosen to enhance her beauty, not place it on blatant display like...

He took another pull of the beer can. Up above his head the hot Spanish sun was burning into his naked shoulders. It felt good enough to have him flexing deep-bedded muscles wrapped in rich brown skin.

Recalling Isobel, he felt a different kind of bite tug at his senses. This one hit him low down in his gut where the sex thing lurked. He grimaced, wondering if or when he would ever want another woman the way he'd wanted Isobel? And hoped he never had to suffer those primitive urges again.

They had gone into marriage like two randy teenagers, loving each other with a passion that had them tearing each other to pieces by the time they'd separated. He had been too young—she had been too young. They'd made love like animals and fought in the same ferocious way until—inevitably probably—it had all turned so nasty and bitter and bad that it had been easier to lock it all away and forget he had a wife than to risk allowing it all to break out again.

But, like his sojourn in San Estéban, it was over now—time to move on with his life. He was thirty-one years old and ready to settle down with a *proper* wife, maybe even a family...

'Why the frown?'

Diantha had come up beside him without him noticing. Turning his head, he looked down into warm brown eyes, saw the soft smile on her lips...and thought of a different smile. This mouth didn't smile, it pouted—provokingly. And those intense green eyes were never warm but just damned defiant.

'I am attempting to come to terms with the fact that it is time for me to leave here,' he answered her question.

'And you do not want to leave,' Diantha murmured understandingly.

Leandros sighed. 'I have come to love this place,' he confessed, looking outwards towards San Estéban again.

There followed a few moments of silence between them, the kind that allowed his mind to drift without intrusion across the empty years during which he had hidden away here, learning to be whole again. San Estéban had been his sanctuary in a time of misery and disillusionment. Isobel had—

It took the gentle touch of Diantha's fingers to his warm bicep to remind him that she was here. They rarely touched. It was not yet that kind of relationship. She was his sister Chloe's closest friend and he was honour-bound to treat her as such while she was here. But his senses stirred in response to those cool fingers—only to settle down again the moment they were removed.

'You know what I think, Leandros,' she said gently. 'I think you have been here for too long. Living the life of a lotus-eater has made you lazy—which makes it a good time for you to return to Athens and move on with your life, don't you think?'

'Ah, words of wisdom,' he smiled. It was truly uncanny how Diantha could tap in to his thinking. 'Don't worry,' he said. 'After the San Estéban celebration I have every intention of returning to Athens and…move on, as you call it,' he promised.

'Good,' she commended. 'Your mama will be pleased to hear it.'

And with that simple blessing she moved away again, walking gracefully back into the stateroom in her neat blue dress that suited her figure and with her glossy black hair coiled with classical Greek conservatism to the slender curve of her nape.

But she did so with no idea that she had left behind her a man wearing another frown because he was seeing long, straight, in-your-face red hair flowing down a narrow spine in a blazing defiance to everything Greek. Isobel would have rather died than wear that neat blue dress, he mused grimly. She preferred short skirts that showed her amazing legs off and skinny little tops that tantalised the eyes with the thrust of her beautiful, button-tipped breasts.

Isobel would rather have cut out her tongue than show concern for his mother's feelings, he mentally added as he turned away again and took another grim pull of his beer. Isobel and his family had not got on. They had rubbed each other up the wrong way from the very beginning, and both factions hadn't attempted to hide that from him.

Diantha, on the other hand, adored his mother and his mother adored her. Being such a close friend to his sister, Chloe, she had always hovered on the periphery of his life, though he had only truly taken notice of her since she had arrived here a week ago to step into the breach to help organise next week's celebration because Chloe, who should have been here helping him, had become deeply embroiled in Nikos's wedding preparations.

It had been good of Diantha in the circumstances. He appreciated the time she had placed at his disposal, particularly since she had only just returned to Athens, having spent the last four years with her family living in Washington, D.C. She was well bred and well liked—her advantages were adding up, he noted. And, other than for a brief romance with his brother Nikos to blot her copybook, she was most definitely much more suitable than that witch of a redhead with sharp barbs for teeth.

With that final thought on the subject he took a final pull of his beer can, saw a man across the quay taking photographs of the yacht and frowned at him. He had a distinct dislike of photographers, not only because they intruded on his privacy but also because it was what his dear wife did for a living. When they had first met she had been aiming a damned camera at him—or was it the red Ferrari he had been leaning against? No, it had been him. She had got him to pose then flirted like mad with him while the camera clicked. By the end of the same day they'd gone to bed, and after that—

He did not want to think about what had happened after that. He did not want to think of Isobel at all. She no longer belonged in his thoughts, and it was about time that he made that official.

The man with the camera turned away. So did Leandros, decisively. He suddenly felt a lot better about leaving here and went inside to…move on with his life.

Isobel's own thinking was moving very much along the same lines as she sat reading the letter that had just arrived from her estranged husband's lawyer giving her notice of Leandros's intention to begin divorce proceedings.

She was sitting alone at a small kitchen table. Her mother hadn't yet risen from her bed. She was glad about that because the letter had come as a shock, even though she agreed with its content. It was time, if not well overdue that one of them should take the bull by the horns and call an official end to a marriage that should have never been.

But the printed words on the page blurred for a moment at the realisation that this was it, the final chapter of a four-year mistake. If she agreed to Leandros's terms, then she knew she would be accepting that those years had been nothing but wasted in her life.

Did he feel the same? Was that why he had taken so long to get to this? It was hard to acknowledge that you could be so fallible, that you had once been stupid enough to let your heart rule your head.

Or was there more to it than a decision to put an end to their miserable marriage? Had he found someone with whom he felt he could spend the rest of his life?

The idea shouldn't hurt but it did. She had loved Leandros so badly at the beginning that she suspected she'd gone a little mad. They'd been young—too young—but oh, it had been so wildly passionate.

Then—no, don't think about the passion, she told herself firmly, and made herself read the letter again.

It was asking her if she would consider travelling to Athens to meet with her husband—in the presence of their respective lawyers, of course—so they could thrash out a settlement in an effort to make the divorce quick and trouble-free. A few days of her time should be enough, Takis Konstantindou was predicting. All expenses would be paid by Leandros for both herself and her lawyer as a goodwill gesture, because Mr Petronades couldn't travel to England at this time.

She paused to wonder why Leandros couldn't travel. For the man she remembered virtually lived out of a suitcase, so it was odd to think of him under some kind of restraint.

It was odd to think about him at all, she extended, and the letter lost its holding power as she sat back in the chair. They'd first met by accident right here in England at an annual car exhibition. She'd been there in her official capacity as photographer for a trendy new magazine—a bright and confident twenty-two-year-old who believed the whole world was at her feet. While he was dashing and twenty-seven years old, with the looks and the build of a genuine dark Apollo.

They'd flirted over the glossy bonnet of some prohibitively expensive sports car. With his looks and his charm and his immaculate clothing, she'd assumed he was one of the car's sales representatives, since they all looked and dressed like a million dollars. It had never occurred to her that far from selling the car they were flirting across he owned several of them. Realisation about just who Leandros was had come a lot later—much too late to do anything about it.

By then he'd already bowled her over with his dark good looks and easy charm and the way he looked at her that left her in no doubt as to what was going on behind his handsome façade. They'd made a date to share dinner and ended up falling into bed at the first opportunity they were handed. His finding out that he was her first lover had only made the passion burn all the more. He'd adored playing the role of tutor. He'd taught her to understand the pleasures of her own body and made sure that she understood what pleasured his. When it came time for him to go back to Greece he'd refused to go without her. They'd married in a hasty civil ceremony then rushed to the airport to catch their flight.

It was as he'd led her onto a private jet with the Petronades logo shining in gold on its side that she started to ask questions. He'd thought it absolutely hilarious that she didn't know she'd married the modern equivalent of Croesus, and had carried her off to the tiny private cabin, where he'd made love to her all the way to Athens. She had never been so happy in her entire life.

But that was it—the sum total of the happy side of their marriage was encapsulated in a single hop from England to Greece. By the time they'd arrived at his family home the whole, whirling wonder of their love was already turning stale. 'You can't wear that to meet my mother;' his first criticism of her could still ring antagonistic bells in her head.

'Why, what's wrong with it?'

'The skirt is too short; she will have a fit. And can you not tie your hair up or something, show a little respect for the people you are about to meet?'

She had not tied her hair up, nor had she changed her clothes. But she had soon learned the hard way that stubborn defiance was one thing when it was aimed at a man who virtually salivated with desire for you even as he criticised. But it was not the same as being boxed and tagged a cheap little floozy at first horrified glance.

Things had gone from bad to worse after that. And—yes, she reiterated as her gaze dipped back to the letter, it *was* time that one of them took the initiative and drew the final curtain across something that should never have been.

In fact, Isobel had only one problem with the details Takis Konstantindou had mapped out in the letter. She could not see how she could spend several days in Athens because she could not leave her mother on her own for that long.

'What time does her flight come in?'

Leandros was sitting at his desk in his plush Athens office. In the two weeks he had been back here he had changed into a different person. Gone was the laid-back man of San Estéban and in his place sat a sharp-edged, hard-headed Greek tycoon.

Was he happy with that? No, he was not happy to become this person again, but needs must when the devil drives, so they said. In this case the devil was the amount of importance other people placed on his time and knowledge. His desk was virtually groaning beneath the weight of paperwork that apparently needed his attention as a matter of urgency. He moved from important meeting to meeting with hardly a breath in between. His social life had gone from a lazy meal eaten in a restaurant on the San Estéban boulevard, to a constant round of social engagements that literally set his teeth on edge. If he lifted his eyes someone jumped to speak to him. If he closed those same eyes someone else would ensure that he opened them again. The wheels of power ground on and on for twenty-four hours of every day and the whole merry-go-round was made all the more intense because his younger brother Nikos was off limits while he prepared for his wedding day.

On his father's death Leandros had become the head of the Petronades family, therefore it was his duty to play host in his father's stead. His mother was becoming more neurotic the closer it came to Nikos's big day, and was likely to panic if she did not have an open line to her eldest son's ear. If he complained she told him not to spoil this for her then reminded him that he had denied her the opportunity to stand proud and watch him make his own disastrous union. And because thoughts of marriage were already on his mind, he was hard put not to snap at her that maybe Nikos could take a leaf out of his own book and run away to marry secretly. At least the day would belong only to him and Carlotta. If there was anything about his own marriage he could still look back on with total pleasure, it was that moment when Isobel had smiled up at him as he placed the ring upon her finger and whispered, 'I love you so much.' He had not needed five hundred witnesses to help prove that vow to be true.

His heart gave him a punishing twinge of regret for what he had once had and lost.

'This evening.' Takis Konstantindou pulled him back from where he had been in danger of visiting. 'But she insisted on making her own arrangements,' Takis informed him. 'She will be staying at the Apollo near Piraeus.'

Leandros frowned. 'But that is a mediocre place with a low star rating. Why should she want to stay there when she could have had a suite at the Athenaeum?'

Takis just shrugged his lack of an answer. 'All I know is that she refused our invitation to make arrangements for her and reserved three rooms, not two, at the Apollo, one of which must have wheelchair access.'

Wheelchair access? Leandros sat forward, his attention suddenly riveted. 'Why?' he demanded. 'What's wrong with her? Has she been hurt…is she ill?'

'I don't know if the special room *is* for her,' Takis answered. 'All I know is that she has reserved such a room.'

'Then find out!' he snapped. Suddenly the thought of his beautiful Isobel trapped in a wheelchair made him feel physically ill!

He must even have gone pale because Takis was looking at him oddly. 'It could change everything, do you not see that?' His tycoon persona jumped to his rescue. 'The whole structure on which we have based our proposals for a settlement may need to be revised to take into account a physical disability.'

'I think you have adequately covered for any such eventuality, Leandros.' The lawyer smiled cynically.

'*Adequate* is not good enough.' He was suddenly furious. 'Adequate is not what I was aiming towards! I am no skinflint! I have no wish to play games with this! Isobel is my wife.' Hearing that 'is' leaving his lips forced him to stop and take a breath. 'I will leave my marriage with no sense of triumph at its failure, Takis,' he informed the other man. 'But I will hopefully leave it with the knowledge that I treated her fairly in the end.'

Takis was looking surprised at his outburst. 'I'm sorry, Leandros, I never meant to—'

'I know what you meant,' he interrupted curtly. 'And I

know what you think.' Which was why that derisory comment about Isobel being *adequately* compensated had made him see red. He knew what his family thought about Isobel. He knew that they probably discussed her between themselves in that same derogatory way. He had even let them—if only by pretending it wasn't happening. But they were wrong if they believed his failed marriage was down to Isobel, because it wasn't. Not all of it anyway.

Takis was wrong about him if he believed that he was filing for divorce because he no longer cared about Isobel. He might not want her back to run riot through his life again, but... 'Whatever anyone else thinks about my marriage to Isobel, she deserves and *will* get my full honour and respect at all times. Do you understand that?'

'Of course.' For a man who was twice his own age and also his godfather, Takis Konstantindou suddenly looked very much the wary employer as he gave a nod of his silvered head. 'It never crossed my—'

'Find out what you can before we meet with her,' Leandros interrupted, glanced at his watch and was relieved to see he was due at a meeting elsewhere so could end this conversation.

He stood up. Takis took his cue without further comment and went off to do his bidding. Leandros waited until the door closed behind him, then threw himself back down into his chair. He knew he was behaving irrationally. He understood why Takis no longer understood just where it was he was coming from. Only two weeks ago Leandros had called up his godfather and informed him he wanted to file for divorce. It had been a brief and unemotional conversation to which Takis had responded in the same brisk, lawyer-like way.

But a few weeks ago, in his head, Isobel had been a witch and a hellion with barbs for teeth. Now, on the back of one small comment she was the young and vulnerable creature he had dragged by the scruff of her beautiful neck out of sensual heaven into the hell of Athenian society.

On a thick oath he stood up again, paced around his desk. What was going on here? he asked himself. What was the matter with him? Did he have to come over all macho and feel suddenly protective because there was a chance that the Isobel he would meet tomorrow was going to be a shadow of the one he once knew?

A wheelchair.

Another oath escaped him. The phone on his desk began to ring. It was Diantha, gently reminding him that his mother would prefer him not to be late for dinner tonight. The tension eased out of his shoulders, her soft, slightly amused tone showing sympathy with his present plight where his mother was concerned. By the time the conversation ended he was feeling better—much more like his gritty, calm self.

Yes, he confirmed. Diantha was good for him. She refocused his mind on those things that should matter, like the meeting he should be attending right now.

'You're asking for trouble dressed like that,' Silvia Cunningham announced in her usual blunt manner.

Isobel took a step back to view herself in the mirror. 'Why, what's wrong with it?' All she saw was a perfectly acceptable brown tailored suit with a skirt that lightly hugged her hips and thighs to finish at a respectable length just below her slender knees. The plain-cut zip-up jacket stopped at her waist and beneath it she wore a staunchly conventional button-through cream blouse. Her hair was neat, caught up in a twist and held in place by a tortoise-shell comb. She was wearing an unremarkable flesh-coloured lipstick, a light dusting of eye-shadow and some black mascara, but that was all.

In fact she could not look more conservative if she tried to be, she informed that hint of a defiant glint she could see burning in her green eyes.

'What's wrong with that suit is that it's an outright provocation,' her mother said. 'The wretched man never could keep his hands off you at the worst of times. What do you think he's going to want to do when you turn up wearing a suit with a definite slink about it?'

'I can't help my figure!' Isobel flashed back defensively. 'It's the one you gave to me, along with the hair and the eyes.'

'And the temper,' Silvia nodded. 'And the wilful desire to let him see what it is he's passing up.'

'Passing up?' Those green eyes flashed. 'Do I have to remind you that I was the one who left him three years ago?'

'And he was the one who did not bother to come and drag you back again.'

Rub it in, why don't you? Isobel thought. 'I haven't got time for this,' she said and began searching for her handbag. 'I have a meeting to go to.'

'You shouldn't be going to this meeting at all!'

'Please don't start again.' Isobel sighed. They had already been through this a hundred times.

'I agree that it is time to end your marriage, Isobel,' her mother persisted none the less, 'and I am even prepared to admit that the letter from Leandros's lawyer brought the best news I'd heard in two long years!'

Looking at the way her mother was struggling to stand with the aid of her walking frame, Isobel understood where she was coming from when she said that.

'But I still think you should have conducted this business through a third party,' she continued, 'and, looking at the way you've dressed yourself up, I am now absolutely positive that coming face to face with him is a mistake!'

'Sit down—please,' Isobel begged. 'Your arms are shaking. You know what they said about overdoing it.'

'I will sit when you stop being so pig-stubborn about this!'

A grin suddenly flashed across Isobel's face. 'Pot calling the kettle black,' she said.

Her mother's mouth twitched. If Isobel ever wanted to know where she got her stubbornness from then she only had to look at Silvia Cunningham. The hair, the eyes, even her strength of will came from this very determined woman. Though all of those features in her mother had taken a severe battering over the last two years since a dreadful car accident. Silvia was recovering slowly, but the damage to her spine had been devastating. Fortunately— and her mother was one for counting her blessings—her mind was still as bright as a polished button and unwaveringly determined to get her full mobility back.

But Sylvia had a tendency to overdo it. Only a few weeks ago she had taken a bad fall. She hadn't broken anything but she'd bruised herself and severely shaken her confidence. It had also shaken Isobel's confidence about leaving her alone throughout the day while she was at work. Then Leandros's letter had arrived to make life even more complicated. It had been easier to just bring Silvia with her than to leave her behind then worry sick for every minute she was away from her.

On a tut of impatience Isobel went to catch up the nearest chair and settled it behind her mother's legs. Silvia lowered herself into it without protest, which said a lot about how difficult she'd been finding it to stand. But that was her mother, Isobel thought as she bent to kiss her smooth cheek. She was a fighter. The fact that she was still of this world and able to hold her own in an argument was proof of it.

'Look,' Isobel said, coming down to her mother's level and moving the walking frame out of the way so that she could claim her hands. 'All right, I confess that I've dressed like this for a reason. But it has nothing to do with trying to make Leandros regret this divorce.' It went much deeper than that, and her darkened eyes showed it. 'He did nothing but criticise my taste in clothes. When he did, I was just too stubborn to make even one small concession to his opinion of what his wife should look like, wear or behave.'

'Quite right too.' Her beautiful, loyal mother nodded. 'Pretentious oaf.'

'Well, I mean to show him that when I have the freedom to choose what the heck I want to wear, then I can be as conventional as anyone.'

A pair of shrewd old eyes looked into their younger matching pair, and saw cracks a mile wide in those excuses just waiting for her daughter to fall right in.

A knock sounded at the door. It would be Lester Miles, Isobel's lawyer. With a hurried smile, Isobel got up to leave. But her mother refused to let go of her hand.

'Don't let him hurt you again,' she murmured urgently.

Isobel's sudden flash of annoyance took Silvia by surprise. 'Whatever else Leandros did to me, he *never* set out to hurt me, Mother.' *Mother* said it all. For Silvia was *Mum* or *sweetheart*, but only ever *Mother* when she was out of line. 'We were in love, but were wrong for each other. Learning to accept that was painful for us both.'

Silvia held her tongue in check and accepted a second kiss on her cheek while Isobel wondered what the heck she was doing defending a man whose treatment of her had been so indefensible!

What was the matter with her? Was it nerves? Was she more stressed about this meeting than she was prepared to admit? Hurt her? What else could Leandros do that could hurt her more than he'd already done three years ago?

Another knock at the door and she was turning towards it, her mind in a sudden hectic whirl. She tried to fight it, tried to stay calm. 'What are you going to do while I'm out?' she asked as she walked towards the door.

'Clive has hired a car. We are going to do some sight-seeing.'

Clive. Isobel's mouth tightened. There was another point of conflict she had not yet addressed. Clive Sanders was their neighbour and very good friend. He was also what Isobel supposed she could call the new man in her life. Or that was what he could be if Isobel gave Clive the green light.

Clive had somehow managed to invite himself along on this trip—aided and abetted by her mother, she was sure. The first she'd known about it was when she'd been in the hotel foyer last night and happened to see him arrive. Clive had just smiled at her burst of annoyance, touched a sooth-ing hand to her angry cheek and said innocently, 'I am here for your mother. You're supposed to be pleased by the surprise, you ungrateful thing.'

But she had been far from pleased or grateful. Too many people seemed to believe they had a right to interfere in her life. Clive insisted the trip to Athens fitted in with his plans for a much-needed break. Her mother insisted it made her feel more secure to have a man like Clive around. Isobel thought there was a conspiracy between the two of them, which involved Clive keeping an eye on her in case she went totally off the rails when she met up with Leandros again.

But she knew differently. For all that she'd just defended Leandros, she knew there was not a single chance that seeing him was going to send her toppling back into the madness of their old love affair. She didn't hate him, but she despised him for the way he had treated her. He'd killed her confidence and her spirit and, finally, her love.

'Don't let him tire you out,' was her clipped comment to Silvia about Clive's presence here.

'He's a fully trained physiotherapist,' Silvia pointed out. 'Give him the benefit of some sense.' Which was her mother's way of making it known that she knew Isobel disapproved of him being here. 'And Isobel,' Silvia added as she was about to pull the door open, 'a brown leather suit is not conventional by any stretch of the imagination, so stop kidding yourself that you're out to do anything but make that man sit up and take note.'

Isobel left the room without bothering to answer, startling Lester Miles with the abruptness with which she appeared. His eyes widened then slid down over the leather suit before carefully hooding in a way that told her he thought her attire inappropriate too.

Maybe it was. Her chin went up. Suddenly she was fizzing like a simmering pot ready to explode because her mother was right—she was out to blow Leandros right out of his shoes.

'Shall we go?' she said.

Lester Miles just nodded and fell into step beside her. He was young and he was eager and she had picked him out at random from the Yellow Pages. Yes, she was dressed for battle, because she didn't think she needed a lawyer to fire her shots for her—though she was happy for him to come along and play the stooge.

For today was redemption day. Today she intended to take back all of those things that Leandros had wrenched from her and walk away a whole person again. She didn't want his money or to discuss *settlements*. She had nothing he could want from her, unless he planned to fight over a gold wedding ring and a few diamond trinkets that had made his mother stare in dismay when she'd found out that her son had given them to Isobel.

Family heirlooms, she recalled. 'A bit wasted on you, don't you think?' his sister Chloe had said. But then, dear Mama and Chloe had not been in the bedroom when the precious heirlooms had been her only attire. They'd not seen the way their precious boy had decked out his wife in every sparkle he could lay his hands on—before he enjoyed the pleasure they gave.

Those same heirlooms still lay languishing in a safety deposit box right here in Athens. Leandros was welcome to them as far as she was concerned. It was going to be interesting to discover just what he was willing to place on the table for their safe return—before she told him she wanted nothing from him, then gave him back his damned diamonds and left with her pride!

The journey across Athens in a taxi took an age in traffic that hardly seemed to move. Lester Miles kept on quizzing her as to what was required of him, but she answered in tight little sentences that gave him no clue at all.

'You are in such a powerful position, Mrs Petronades,' he pointed out. 'With no pre-nuptial agreement you are entitled to half of everything your husband owns.'

Isobel blinked. She hadn't given a single thought to a pre-nuptial agreement or the lack of one, come to that. Was this why Leandros wanted to see her personally? Was he out to charm her into seeing this settlement thing from his point of view? The stakes had quite suddenly risen. A few family heirlooms didn't seem to matter any more when you put them in the giant Petronades pot of gold.

'Negotiations will stand or fall on which of you wants this divorce more,' Lester Miles continued. 'As it was your husband who instigated proceedings, I think we can safely say that power is in your hands.'

'You've done your homework,' she murmured.

'Of course,' he said. 'It is what you hired me to do.'

'Does that mean you might know *why* my husband has suddenly decided he wants this divorce?' she enquired curiously.

'I have not been able to establish anything with outright proof,' the lawyer warned her, then looked so uncomfortable Isobel felt that fizz in her stomach start up again. 'But I do believe there is another woman involved. She goes by the name of Miss Diantha Christophoros. She is from one of the most respected families in Greece, my sources tell me…'

His sources couldn't be more right, Isobel agreed as she shifted restlessly in recognition of the Greek beauty's name. A union between the Petronades and Christophoros families would be the same as founding a dynasty. Mama Petronades must be so very pleased.

'She spent some time with your husband on his yacht recently,' her very efficient lawyer continued informatively. 'Also, your brother-in-law—Nicolas Petronades—will be marrying Carlotta Santorini next week. Rumour has it that once his brother is married your husband would like to follow suit. It could be an heir thing,' he suggested. 'Powerful families like the Petronades prefer to keep the line of succession clear cut.'

An heir thing, Isobel repeated. Felt tears sting the backs of her eyes and the fizz happening inside her turn to an angry ache.

To hell with you, Leandros, she thought bitterly.

CHAPTER TWO

TO HELL with you, Isobel repeated fifteen minutes later, when finally they came face to face in the elegant surroundings of Leondros's company boardroom with all its imposing wood panelling and fancy portraits of past masters.

Here stood the latest in a long line of masters, she observed coldly. Leandros Petronades, lean, dark and as arrogant as ever. A man built to break hearts, as she should know.

He stood six feet two inches tall and wore a grey suit, white shirt and a grey silk tie that drew a line down the length of a torso made up of tensile muscle wrapped in silk-like bronze skin. He hadn't changed, not so much as an inch of him; not the aura of leashed power beneath the designer clothing, or the sleek, handsome structure of his face. His hair was still that let-me-touch midnight-black colour, his eyes dark like the richest molasses ever produced, and his mouth smooth, slim, very masculine—the mouth of a born sensualist.

She wanted to reach out and slap his face. She wanted to leap on him and beat at his adulterous chest with her fists. The anger, the pain, the black, blinding pulse of emotional fury was literally throbbing along her veins. It was as if the last three years hadn't happened. It could have been yesterday that she had walked out of his life. Diantha Christophoros of all women, she was thinking. Diantha, the broken-hearted one who had had to be taken out of

Athens by her family when Leandros arrived there with his shocking new wife.

Did he think she didn't know about her? Did he really believe his awful sister would have passed up the opportunity to let her know what he had thrown away in the name of hot sex? Did he think Chloe would have kept silent about the trips he made to Washington D.C. to visit his broken-hearted ex?

I hate you, her eyes informed him while the anger sang in her blood. She didn't speak, she didn't want to. And as they stared at each other along half the length of his impressive boardroom table the silence screamed like a banshee in everyone's ears. His uncle Takis was there but she refused to look at him. Lester Miles stood somewhere behind her, watchful and silent as the grave. Leandros didn't make a single move to come and greet her, his dark eyes drifting over her as if they were looking at a snake.

Well, that just about says it all, she thought coldly. His family has finally managed to indoctrinate him into their speciality of recognising dross.

Having just watched his wife of four years walk into his boardroom—and scanned her sensational legs—Leandros was held paralysed by the force of anger which roared up inside him like a lion about to leap.

So much for killing himself by imagining her a mere shadow of her former self, he was thinking bitterly. So much for feeling that overwhelming sense of relief when he'd found out it was not Isobel who was confined to a wheelchair but her mother—then feeling the guilt of being relieved about something so painfully tragic, whoever the victim! Silvia Cunningham had been a beautiful woman, full of life and energy. To think of that fine spirit that she had passed on to her daughter now quashed into a wheelchair had touched him deeply.

He was in danger of laughing out loud at his latest plan to make sure that Isobel's mother was provided for within the settlement. Indeed that plan was not about to change because of what he now knew.

Only his plans for this beautiful, adulterous creature standing here in front of him, with her glossed-back hair, spitting green eyes and tight little mouth with its small upper lip and protruding bottom lip that made him want to leap on it and bite.

Where only hours ago he had been content to be unbelievably kind and gentle. He now wanted to tear her limb from limb.

Four years—for four long years this woman had lived inside him like a low, throbbing ache. He'd felt guilt, he'd felt sadness, he'd wanted to accord her the respect he'd believed she deserved from him by making no one aware of his plans to remarry until he had eased himself out of this marriage in the least hurtful way that he could.

But that was until he discovered that his wife was suffering from no such feelings of sensitivity on his behalf, for she had brought her lover with her to Athens! Could she not manage for two days without the oversized brute? Did he satisfy her, did he know her as intimately as he did? Could he make her tremble from her toes to her fingertips and cry out and grab for him as she reached her peak?

Cold fury sparked from his eyes as he looked her over. Bitterness raked its claws across his face. She was wearing leather. Why leather? What was it she was aiming to prove here, that she was brazen enough to wear such a fabric—bought with his money, no doubt—but worn to please another man?

'You're late,' he incised, flicking hard eyes up to a face that was even more treacherously perfect than he remembered it. The gentle hairline, the dark-framed eyes, the straight little nose and that provoking little mouth. A mouth that knew how to kiss a man senseless, how to latch on to his skin and drive him out of his mind. He'd seen the oversized blond brute with the affable smile, standing in the hotel foyer wearing cotton sweats and touching her as if he had every right.

He should not have gone there. He should not have been so anxious to find out the truth about the wheelchair, then he would not have had to witness that man touching his wife in full view of anyone who wanted to watch.

His wife! Touching *his* wife's exquisite, smooth white skin, making that skin flush when it only used to flush like that for him! She had not been wearing leather then, but tight jeans and a little white top that showed the fullness of her beautiful breasts!

Her wonderful hair had been flowing down her back, not pinned up as if she was some little prude. A lying prude, he extended.

'This meeting was due to begin fifteen minutes ago. Now we will have to keep it brief,' he finished his cutting comment.

Then watched as her witch's green eyes narrowed at his clipped, tight tone. 'The traffic was bad—'

'The traffic in Athens is always bad,' he inserted dismissively. 'You have not been away from this city for so long that you could have forgotten that. Please take a seat.'

He took a seat. He pulled out a chair at random and threw himself into it with a force that verged on insolence. Takis was frowning at him but he ignored this lawyer's expression. The other lawyer was trying not to show anything, though Leondros could see he was thoroughly engrossed.

Perhaps fascinated was a better word, he decided as he

studied his wife's lawyer through glassed-over eyes. The man was nothing but a young hawk, still wet behind the ears, he noted with contempt. What was Isobel thinking about, putting a guy like this up against himself and Takis? She knew of his godfather's brutal reputation, she knew of his own! The only thing that Lester Miles seemed to have going for him was the cut of his suit and his boyish good looks.

Maybe that was it, he then thought with a tightening of just about every nerve. Maybe the body-builder was not her only man. Maybe this guy held a different place in her busy private life.

Irritation with himself made him take out his silver pen and begin tapping it against the polished boardroom table while he waited for this meeting to begin. Takis was shaking hands with Lester Miles and trying to appear as if Isobel's husband always behaved like this. Isobel, on the other hand, was walking on those long legs down the length of the boardroom table on the opposing side to his. The leather suit stretched against her slender thighs as she moved and the jacket moulded to the thrust of her breasts. Was she wearing anything beneath it? Did she have the jacket zipped up to her throat simply to taunt him with that question?

Her chin was set, her flesh so white and smooth it didn't look real—but then it never had. She chose to take the seat right opposite him. As she pulled the chair out his gaze moved to the smooth length of her slender neck, then up to the perfect shell-like shape of her ear, and his teeth came together with a snap. One cat-like lick of that ear and all of that cool composure would melt like wax to her dainty feet, he mused lusciously. He knew her, he knew her likes and dislikes, he knew every single erogenous zone, had been the one to take her on that journey of glorious discovery. He knew how to make her beg, cling, cry out his name in a paroxysm of ecstasy. Give him two minutes alone with her and he could wipe away that icy exterior; give him another minute and he could have her naked and begging for him. Or maybe he should be the one to strip his clothes off, he mused grimly. Maybe he should take her on the ride of their lives up against the panelled wall, with her skirt hitched up just high enough for his flesh to enjoy the erotic slide against leather while other parts of him enjoyed a different kind of slide, inside the hot, moist core of her ever-eager body.

It was almost a shame that he wasn't into sexual enhancers, though it suddenly occurred to him that the body-builder looked the type. A new and blistering flash of his recently constructed fantasy now being enacted by the lover sent his eyes black with rage.

She sat down, bent to place her handbag on the floor by her chair, then sat up straight again—and looked him right in the eye. Hostility slammed into his face. His pulse quickened as the glinting green look lanced straight through him and war was declared. Though he wasn't sure which of them had done the declaring.

She had certainly arrived here ready for a battle, though why that was the case he had no idea. It was not as if *he* had done anything other than suggest this divorce. Since it was very clear that she had not spent the last three years pining for him, her hostility was, in his opinion, without cause.

Whereas his own hostility... His narrowed eyes shot warning sparks across the table. She lifted her chin to him and sent the sparks right back. His fingers began to tingle with an urge to do something—they began tapping the pen all the harder against the polished table-top.

What is it you think you are going to get out of this,

you faithless little hellion? he questioned silently as his lips parted to reveal the tight, warning glint of clenched white teeth. You had better be well prepared for this fight, because I am.

She placed her hands down on the table, long white fingers tipped with pink painted fingernails stroked the polished wood surface like a caress. His loins tightened, his chest began to burn. She saw it happen and her upper lip offered a derogatory curl.

Takis took the chair beside him. Lester Miles sat down beside Isobel. She turned to her lawyer and sent him a smile that would have made an iceberg melt. But Lester Miles was no iceberg. As he watched this little byplay, Leandros saw the young fool's cheekbones streak with colour as he sent an answering smile in return.

It's OK, I am here, that smile said to her. Leandros felt the lion inside him roar again. She turned to fix her gaze back on him. I am going to kill you, he told her silently. I am going to reach out and drag you across this table and spoil your little piece of foreplay with the kind of real play that shatters the mind.

'Shall we begin?' Takis opened a blue folder. Lester Miles had a black leather one, smooth, trendy and upwardly mobile. Isobel slid her hands to her lap.

Leandros continued to tap his pen against the desk.

'In the midst of all of this tension, may I begin by assuring you, Isobel, that we have every desire to keep this civil and fair?'

Leandros watched her shift her gaze from his face to Takis. He felt the loss deep in his gut. 'Hello, Uncle Takis,' she said.

It was a riveting moment. Takis froze, so did Lester Miles, glancing up sharply from his trendy black leather dossier to sniff the new tension suddenly eddying in the air. The deeply respected international lawyer of repute, Takis Konstantindou, actually blushed.

He came back to his feet. 'My sincere apologies, Isobel,' he murmured uncomfortably. 'How could I have been so crass as to forget my manners?'

'That's OK,' she replied and, as Takis was about to stretch across the table to offer her his hand, she returned her eyes back to Leandros, leaving Takis suffering the indignity of lowering his hand and returning to his seat.

So she could still twist a room upon its head without effort, Leandros noted. You bitch, he told her silently.

The mocking movement of a slender eyebrow said— Maybe I am, but at least I won't be your bitch for much longer.

The air began to crackle. 'As I was about to say...' clearing his throat, Takis tried again '...with due regard to the sensitivities of both parties, at my client's instruction I have drawn up a draft copy of proposals to help ease us through this awkward part.' Taking out a sheet of paper, he slid it across the table towards Isobel. She didn't even glance at it, but left Lester Miles to pick it up and begin to read. 'As I think you will agree, we have tried to be more than fair in our proposals. The financial settlement is most generous in the circumstances.'

'What circumstances?' her lawyer questioned.

Takis looked up. 'Our clients have not lived together for three years,' he explained.

Three years, one month and twenty-four days, Isobel amended silently, and wished Leandros would stop tapping that pen. He was looking at her as if she was his worst enemy. The tight mouth, the glinting teeth, the ice picks flicking out from stone-cold black eyes, all told her he could not get rid of her quick enough.

It hurt, though she knew it shouldn't. It hurt to see the

way he had been running those eyes over her as if he could not believe he'd ever desired someone like her. So much for dressing for the occasion, she mused bleakly. So much for wanting to blow him out of his handmade shoes.

Lester Miles nodded. 'Thank you,' he said and returned his attention to the list in front of him, and Takis returned to reading out loud the list of so-called provisions. Isobel wanted to be sick. Did they think that material goods were all she was here for? Did Leandros truly believe she was so mercenary?

'When,' she tossed at him, 'did I ever give you the impression that I was a greedy little gold-digger?'

Black lashes that were just too long for a man lifted away from his eyes. 'You are here, are you not?' he countered smoothly. 'What other purpose could you have in mind?'

Isobel stiffened as if he'd shot her. He was implying that she was either here for the money or to try to win him back.

'Both parties have stated that the breakdown in their marriage was due to—irreconcilable differences,' Takis put in swiftly. 'I see nothing to be gained from attempting to apportion blame now. Agreed?'

'Agreed,' Lester Miles said.

But Isobel didn't agree. She stared at the man she had married and thought about the twenty-three hours in any given day when he'd preferred to forget he had a wife. Then, during the twenty-fourth, he'd found it infuriating when she'd chosen to refuse to let him use it to assuage his flesh!

He'd met her, lusted after her, then married her in haste to keep her in his bed. The sex had been amazing, passionate and hot, but when he had discovered there was more to marriage than just sex, he had repented at his leisure *during* the year it had taken her to commit the ultimate sin in the eyes of everyone—by getting pregnant.

Leandros must be the only Greek man who could be horrified at this evidence of his prowess. How the hell did it happen? he'd raged. Don't you think we have enough problems without adding a baby to them? Two and a half months later she'd miscarried and he could not have been more relieved. She was too young. He wasn't ready. It was for the best.

She hated him. It was all coming back to her how much she did. She even felt tears threatening. Leandros saw them and the pen suddenly stopped its irritating tap.

'Your client left my client of her own volition,' Takis was continuing to explain to Lester Miles while the two of them became locked in an old agony. 'And there has been no attempt at contact since.'

Yes, you bastard, Isobel silently told Leandros. You couldn't even bother to come and find out if I was miserable. Not so much as a letter or a brief phone call to check that I was alive!

'By either party?' Lester Miles questioned.

The pen began to tap again, Leandros's lips pressing together in a hardening line. He didn't care, Isobel realised painfully. He did not want to remember those dark hours and days and weeks when she'd been inconsolable and he had been too busy with other things to deal with an over-emotional wife.

'Mr Petronades pays a respectable allowance into Mrs Petronades' account each month but I do not recall Mrs Petronades acknowledging it,' Takis said.

'I don't want your money,' Isobel sliced across the table at Leandros. 'I haven't touched a single penny of it.'

'Not my problem,' he returned with an indifferent shrug. 'Now we come to the house in Hampshire, England,'

Takis determinedly pushed on. 'In the interests of goodwill this will be signed over to Mrs Petronades as part of the—'

'I don't want your house, either,' she told Leandros.

'But—Mrs Petronades. I don't—'

'You will take the house,' Leandros stated without a single inflexion.

'As a conscience soother for yourself?'

His eyes narrowed. 'My conscience is clear,' he stated.

She sat back in her chair with a deriding scoff. He dropped the pen then snaked forward in his chair, his black eyes still fixed on her face. 'But why don't you tell me about your conscience?' he invited.

'Leandros, I don't think this is getting us—'

'Keep your house,' Isobel repeated. 'And keep whatever else you've put on that list.'

'You want nothing from me?'

'Nothing—' Isobel took the greatest pleasure in confirming.

'Nothing that is on this list!' Lester Miles quickly jumped in as a fresh load of tension erupted around them. Leandros was looking dangerous, and Isobel was urging him on. Takis was running a fingertip around the edge of his shirt collar because he knew what could happen when these two people began taking bites out of each other.

'Mrs Petronades did not sign a pre-nuptial agreement,' Lester Miles continued hurriedly. 'Which means that she is entitled to half of everything her husband owns. I see nothing like that amount listed here. I think we should...'

Leandros flashed Lester Miles a killing glance. If the young fool did not keep his mouth shut he would help him. 'I was not speaking to you,' he said and returned his gaze to Isobel. 'What is it is that you do want?' he prompted.

Like antagonists in a new cold war they faced each other

across the boardroom table. Anger fizzed in Isobel's brain, and bitterness—a blinding, stinging, biting hostility—had her trembling inside. He had taken her youth and optimism and crushed them. He had taken her love and shredded it before her eyes. He had taken her right to feel worthy as the mother of his child and laughed at it. Finally, he had taken what was left of her pride and been glad to see the back of her.

She'd believed there was nothing else he could do to hurt her. She'd actually come here to Athens ready to let go of the past and leave again hopefully feeling whole. But no. If just one name had the ability to crush her that bit more, then it would be that of Diantha Christophoros.

For that name alone, if she only could reach him she would scratch his eyes out; if she could wrestle him to the ground she would trample all over him in her spike heels.

But she had to make do with lancing him with words. 'I don't want your houses, and I don't want your money,' she informed him. 'I don't want your name or you, come to that. I don't even want your wedding ring...' Wrenching it off her finger, she slid it across the table towards him, then bent and with a snatch caught up her bag. 'And I certainly don't want your precious family heirlooms,' she added, holding her three witnesses silent as she took a sealed envelope out of the bag and launched it to land beside the ring. 'In there you will find the key to my safety deposit box, plus a letter authorising you to empty it for yourself,' she informed Leandros. 'Give them to your next wife,' she suggested. 'They might not be wasted on her.'

Leandros did not look anywhere but at her face while she spat her replies at him. 'So I repeat,' he persisted, 'what is it that you do want?'

'A divorce!' she lanced back through tear-burned eyes. 'See how much you are worth to me, Leandros? All I want is a nice quick divorce from you so that I can put you right out of my life!'

'Insult me one more time, and you might not like the consequences,' he warned very thinly.

'What could you do to me that you haven't already done?' she laughed.

Black eyes turned into twin lasers. 'Show you up for the tramp you are by bringing your muscle-building lover into this?'

For a moment Isobel did not know what he was talking about. Then she issued a stifled gasp. 'You've been having me watched!' she accused.

'Guilty as charged,' he admitted and sat back indolently, picked up the pen again and began weaving it between long brown fingers. 'Adultery is an ugly word,' he drawled icily. 'I could drag you, your pride and your lover through the courts if you wish to turn this into something nasty.'

Nasty. It had *always* been nasty since the day she'd married him. 'Do it, then,' she invited. 'I still won't accept a single Euro from you.'

With that she stood up and, to both lawyers' deepening bewilderment, snatched up her bag and turned to leave.

'Isobel, please—' It was Takis who tried to appeal to her.

'Mrs Petronades, please think about this—?' Lester Miles backed him up.

'Get out of here, the pair of you,' Leandros cut across the two other men. 'Take one more step towards that door, Isobel, and you know I will drag you back and pin you down if necessary.'

Her footsteps slowed to a reluctant standstill. She was trembling so badly now she actually felt sick. In the few seconds of silence that followed she actually wondered if the two lawyers were about to caution him.

But no, they weren't that brave. He was bigger than them in every way a man could be. Height, size—bloody ego. They both slunk past her with their heads down, like two rats deserting a sinking ship.

The door closed behind them. They were alone now. She spun on her slender heels, her eyes like glass. 'You are such a bully,' she said in disgust.

'Bully.' He pulled a face. 'And you, my sweet, are such an angelic soul.'

The *my sweet* stiffened her backbone. He had only ever used the endearment to mock or taunt. He was still flicking that wretched pen around in his fingers. His posture relaxed like a big cat taking its ease. But she wasn't fooled. His mouth was thin, his eyes glinting behind those carefully lowered eyelashes, his jaw rigid, teeth set. He was so angry he was literally pulsing with it beneath all of that idleness.

'Tell me about Clive Sanders.'

There was the reason for it.

She laughed, it was that surreal. He dared to demand an explanation from her after three years of nothing? Walking back to the table, she leaned against it, placed the flat of her palms on its top then looked him hard in the face. 'Sex,' she lied. 'I'm good at it, if you recall. Clive thinks so too. He…'

The table was no obstacle. He was around it before she could say another word. The cat-like analogy had not been conjured up out of nowhere; when he pounced he did it silently. In seconds she was lying flat on her back with him on top of her, and in no seconds at all she was experiencing a different kind of sensation.

This one involved his touch and his weight and his lean, dark features looming so close that her tongue actually moistened with an urge to taste. It was awful. Memories of never holding back whenever he was this close. Memories of passion and desire and need neither had bothered to hold in check.

'Say that again, from this position,' he gritted.

'Get off me.' In desperation she began pushing hard against his shoulders, but the only things that moved were her clenched fists slipping against the smooth cloth of his jacket. She could feel the heat of his body, its power and its promise.

'Say it!' he rasped.

Her eyes flashed like green lightning bolts filled with contempt for everything he stood for. His anger, his arrogance, his ability to make her feel like this. 'I don't have to *do* anything for you any more, *ever*,' she lashed at him.

He released a hard laugh that poured scorn onto her face. 'Sorry to disappoint you, angel, but you still do plenty for me,' and he gave a thrust of his hips so she would know and understand.

Shock brought the air from her lungs on a shaken whisper. 'You're disgusting,' she gasped.

But no more than she was, when the cradle of her own hips moved in response and that oh, so damning animal instinct to mate dragged a groan from her lungs.

He laughed again, huskily, then reached up to tug the comb from her hair. 'There,' he growled as red fire uncoiled across his fingers, 'now you look more like the little wanton I married. All we need to do now is see how wanton,' and his fingers moved down to deal with the jacket zip. The leather slid apart to reveal her neat cream blouse with its pearly buttons up to her throat. Whatever the blouse was supposed to say to him, she did not expect the flaming clash of her eyes with his, as if she'd committed some terrible sin.

'Why the sexy leather?' he demanded. 'Why the prim

hairstyle and a blouse my mother would refuse to wear? What are you trying to prove, Isobel?' he lanced down at her. 'That there are different kinds of sexual provocation? Or is this the way you've learned to dress for your new lover? Does he like to peel you, layer by exquisite layer, is that it?'

'Yes,' she hissed into his hard face. 'The more layers I have on the more I excite him! Whereas you lacked the finesse to notice me at all unless I was already naked in bed and thoroughly convenient for a quick lay!'

The *quick lay* struck right at his ego. Both saw the blistering flashback of his last urgent groping before she'd left him for good. Sparks flew, heat, pain then an anguish that coiled a sound inside his throat.

'You bitch.' The sound arrived in a hoarse whisper.

He'd gone pale and tears were suddenly threatening her again. On a thick whimper she tried to dislodge him with the pushing thrust of her body, making leather squeak against polish wood and the heels of her shoes come close to scoring deep marks in the wood.

'Let me go!' she choked out helplessly. He caught the sound with his mouth and his tongue, and a full onslaught followed of someone who needed to assuage what she had just flung up into his face. Within seconds she had lost the will to fight this man who knew exactly how to kiss her senseless and make her cling with the hungry need for more.

One of his hands was in her hair while the other was sliding between their bodies, making her spine arch sensually as the backs of his knuckles skidded over her breasts. The blouse sprang free, he was that deft with buttons, long fingers slid beneath a final covering of flimsy brown lace and claimed her nipple. She groaned in dismay but was already threading her fingers into his hair as she did so, making sure that he didn't break away.

It was all so primitively, physically *basic*! The harried sound of their laboured breathing, the squeak of leather on polished wood. The heat of his lips and the lick of his tongue and the slow, deep, sinuous thrust of his hips against the eager thrust of her own, that even with the thickness of her skirt was pulling her deeper into a morass of desire. If he reached down and touched the naked flesh at her thighs she would be his for the taking; the tingling already happening there was so tight she could barely stop herself from begging for it.

Suddenly she was free. It happened so quickly that she wasn't expecting it. Dizzy, disorientated, she lay there gasping and blinking as he arrived lightly on his feet by the table and between two chairs. She'd forgotten the anger with which he'd started this. But now she remembered, felt tears of humiliation fill her eyes and didn't even bother to fight him when he took hold of her by the waist, lifted her up and swung her to her trembling feet.

He saw the tears, and a sigh rasped from him. 'I hate you,' she whispered shakily. 'You always were an animal.'

'You should not have brought your lover to Athens!' he ground out. 'You insulted me by doing so!'

She responded by instinct. A hand went up, caught him a hard, stinging slap to the side of his face, then she was grabbing up her bag and turning to walk away. Unsteady legs carried her forward, as her trembling fingers hurriedly tried to zip up her jacket—while her hair flowed down her spine like a red-hot flag that proclaimed what they had been doing.

He didn't stop her, which she took as a further insult. When she arrived in the next room the two lawyers stared at her tear-darkened eyes and dishevelled appearance in open dismay.

'Whatever he wants,' she instructed Lester Miles. 'Have him draw up the papers and I'll sign them.'

With that she just kept on walking.

Leandros had never been so angry with himself in a long time. He'd just treated her like a whore and for what reason?

He didn't have one. Not now that sanity had returned, anyway.

Three years.

He couldn't believe his own crassness! Three years apart and he had reacted to the sight of her with her lover as if he'd caught them red-handed in his own bed! She was young and normal and perfectly healthy. She was beautiful and desirable and she had a sex-drive like anyone else! If she had utilised her right to sleep with another man, then what did that have to do with him now?

It had a great deal to do with him, he grimly countered that question. On a dark and primitively sexual level she still belonged to him. Not once in the last three years had he thought about her taking other lovers. How stupid did that make him? Supremely, so he discovered, because from the moment she'd stepped into this room he'd tossed half a century out of the window to become the jealously possessive Greek male.

Then he remembered the expression in her eyes that had brought with it the memory of the last time they had been together. Something thick lurched in his gut and he reeled violently away from what it was trying to make him feel.

Guilty as charged. An animal lacking the finesse of which he was once so very proud. The boardroom door opened as he was splashing a shot of whisky into a glass.

It was Takis. 'She slapped your face,' the lawyer commented, noticing the finger marks standing out on his cheek. 'I suspect that you deserved it.'

Oh, yes, he'd deserved it, Leandros thought grimly and picked up the glass of whisky then stood staring at it. 'What did she say?' he asked grimly.

'Give him anything he wants,' Takis replied. 'I am to draw up the papers and she will sign them. So take my advice, Leandros, and do it now before she changes her mind. That woman is dangerous. Whatever you did to her here has made her dangerous.'

'She admitted it—to my face—that she's sleeping with that bastard,' he said as if it should explain away everything.

To another Greek male maybe it did in some small part. 'Did you tell her that you want this divorce because you already have her replacement picked out and waiting in the wings to become your wife?'

Shock spun him on his heel to stare at Takis. 'Who told you that?' he demanded furiously.

Takis suddenly looked wary. 'I believe it is common knowledge.'

Common knowledge, Leandros repeated silently. Common knowledge put about by whom? His hopeful mother? His matchmaking sister? Or Diantha herself?

Then, no, not Diantha, he told himself firmly. She is not the kind of woman to spread gossip about. 'Gossip is just that—gossip,' he muttered, more to himself than to Takis. 'Isobel will not be here long enough to hear it.'

Did that matter to him? he then had to ask himself, and sighed when he realised that yes, it mattered to him. What was wrong with him? Another sigh hissed from him. Why was he feeling like this about a woman he hadn't wanted in years?

He detected a pause, one of those telling ones that

grabbed your attention. He glanced at Takis; saw his expression. 'What?' he prompted sharply.

'She knows,' he told him. 'Her lawyer mentioned the Christophoros name before he went after Isobel.'

Leandros felt his mind go blank for a split-second. She cannot know, he tried to convince himself.

'The guy knew quite a lot as a matter of fact,' Takis went on and there was surprise and reluctant respect in the tough lawyer's voice. 'He knew that Diantha spent time alone with you on your yacht in Spain, for instance. He also mentioned conservative attitudes in Greece to extramarital affairs, then suggested we review the kind of scandal it would cause if two big names such as Petronades and Christophoros were linked in this way in a court battle. He's a clever young man,' Takis concluded. 'He needs watching. I might even use him myself one day.'

Leandros was barely listening. His mind had gone off somewhere else. It was seeing Isobel's face when she'd walked in here, seeing the anger, the hate, the desire to tear him to shreds where he stood.

'Dear God,' he breathed. Where had his head been? Why had he not read the signs? When she hurt she came out fighting. Make her feel vulnerable and expendable and she unsheathed her claws. Let her know she wasn't good enough and she spat fire and brimstone over you then ran for cover as quickly as she could. Let her think she was being replaced with one of Athens' noblest, and you could not hurt her more deeply if you tried.

'The lack of a pre-nuptial is beginning to worry me.' Takis was still talking to a lost audience. 'She could take you to the cleaners if she decided she wanted to roll your name in the mud.'

Turning, Leandros looked at the table where the imprint of her body had dulled the polished wood surface. His stomach turned over—not with distaste for what he had done there but for other far more basic reasons. He could still feel the imprint of her down his front, could still taste her in his mouth.

Not far away, resting where it had landed when she tossed them at him, lay her wedding ring and the envelope containing access to the so-called family heirlooms.

What family heirlooms? he thought frowningly. It was not something his family possessed.

Until today she had still worn her wedding ring, even after three years of no contact with him, he mused on while absently twisting his own wedding ring between finger and thumb. Did a woman do that when she took herself a lover? Did she flout convention so openly?

Ah, the lover, he backtracked slightly. The muscle-building blond with the lover's light touch. His senses began to sizzle, his anger returned. Getting rid of the whisky glass, he walked up to the table and picked up the envelope and the ring.

'We need to start moving on this, Leandros,' Takis was prompting him.

'Later,' he said absently.

'Later is not good enough,' the lawyer protested. 'I am telling you as your lawyer that if you want a quick, clean divorce then you have to move now.'

But I don't want a divorce, was the reply that lit up like a halogen light bulb in his head. I want my wife back. *My wife!*

CHAPTER THREE

Out in the street Isobel hailed a passing taxi, gave the driver the name of her hotel then sank back in her seat with a shaking sigh. Maybe she should have waited for Lester Miles to join her but at this precise moment she didn't want anyone witnessing the state she was in.

'You OK, *thespinis*?' the taxi driver questioned.

Glancing up, she saw the driver studying her through his rear-view mirror, his brown eyes clouded by concern.

Did she look that bad?

Yes, she looked that bad, she accepted. Inside she was a mass of shakes and tremors. Beneath her zipped-up jacket her blouse was still gaping open and there wasn't an inch of flesh that wasn't still wearing the hot imprint of a man's knowing touch. Her hair was hanging around her pale face and her mouth was hot, swollen and quivering from the kind of assault that should have set her screaming for help but instead she just—

'Yes—thank you,' she replied and lowered her eyes so he wouldn't see just how big a lie that was.

She felt like a whore. Her eyes filmed over. How could he do that to her? What had she ever done to him to make him believe he had the right to treat her that way?

You riled him into doing it is what happened, a deriding little voice in her head threw in. You went in there wanting to rip his unfaithful heart out and ended up with him ripping out yours!

She stared at the fingers of one hand as they rubbed anxiously at the empty place on another finger where her wedding ring had used to be, and tried to decide if she hurt more because of the way he had just treated her, or because she was still flailing around in the rotten discovery that she was still in love with the over-sexed brute!

It had hit her the moment Lester Miles had mentioned a future wife and Diantha Christophoros in the same, soul-destroying breath. Couldn't he have come up with some-one fresh instead of picking out his old love to replace her with?

He'd also been having her watched, she suddenly re-membered. Had he been that desperate to find a solid rea-son to bring their marriage crashing down that he'd had to go to such extremes?

I hate him, she thought on a blistering wave of agony. And she did. The two opposing emotions of love and ha-tred were swilling around inside her in one gigantic, diz-zying mix. The man was bad for her. He had always been bad for her. Three years on, she thought wretchedly, and her stupid heart had not learned anything!

The taxi pulled into the kerb outside her hotel. Fumbling in her purse, Isobel unearthed some money to pay the driver then climbed out into the heat of a midday sun. Within seconds she felt as if she was melting, which only made a further mockery of her sanity in coming here to Athens at all *and* wearing leather of all things in this city famous for the oppressive weight of its summer heat.

Her mother had been right; she'd been asking for trou-ble—and had certainly found it! Returning to her hotel room, she stripped off the wretched suit and walked into the bathroom to shower his touch from her skin.

Never again, she vowed as she scrubbed with a grim disregard for her skin's fragile layers. By the time she had finished drying herself she was tingling all over for a dif-ferent reason and her mood had altered from feeling destroyed to mulish. If she'd ever needed to be reminded why she left Leandros in the first place then that little scene in his boardroom had done it.

She didn't need a man like him. Let him pour his money into his settlement, she invited, as she dressed in a pair of loose-fitting green cotton trousers and a matching T-shirt. Let him have his divorce so he can marry Diantha Christophoros and produce black-eyed, black-haired little thoroughbreds for his dynasty—

Was that it? Her head shot up, the brush she was using on her hair freezing as she struck at the heart of it. Had Leandros changed his mind about children and decided it was time he made an effort to produce the next Petronades heir?

What was it Lester Miles had said? She tried to remember as she brushed her hair into one long, thick, silken lock. Nikos was getting married. The lawyer called it an heir thing. Nikos might be three years younger than his brother but if Leandros wanted to keep the line of succession clear in his favour, then he needed to get in first with a son.

The tears came back. I would have given him a son. I would have given him a hundred babies if he'd only wanted them. But he didn't, not with me for a mother. He wanted a black-haired Greek beauty with a name exalted enough to match his own.

I'm going to be sick, she thought and had to stand there for a few minutes, fighting the urge as a three-year-old scar ripped open in her chest.

She had to get out of here. The need came with a sudden urgency that left her no room to think. Securing her hair into a simple pony-tail, she snatched up her camera case and slung the strap over her shoulder, slid a pair of sunglasses onto the top of her head then headed for the outer door.

It was only when she stepped out into the hotel corridor that she remembered her mother, and felt guilty because she didn't want to see her right now while she was in this emotional mess. But in all fairness she could not just walk out of here without checking Silvia was back. With a deep breath for courage, she knocked on the door next to her own room. There was no answer. Silvia must still be out with Clive. Relief flicked through her. In the next minute she was riding the lift to the foyer, so eager to escape now that she could barely contain the urge long enough to leave a message for her mother at Reception to let her know what she was doing.

As luck would have it, she was about to step outside when Lester Miles strode in.

'How quickly did they draw up the papers?' she questioned tartly.

'They didn't.' The lawyer frowned. 'Mr Petronades left just after you did.'

To dance attendance on his future bride? Isobel wondered, and felt another burst of bitterness rend a hole in her chest.

'So what happens now?' she asked.

'I am to wait further instruction,' Lester Miles informed her.

'Really?' she drawled. At whose command—Leandros's or Takis Konstantindou's? 'Well, since I am the one you are supposed to take instruction from, Mr Miles, take the afternoon off,' she invited. 'Enjoy a bit of sightseeing and forget about them.'

It was what she intended to do anyway.

'But, Mrs Petronades,' he protested, 'we are due to fly

home tomorrow evening. We really should discuss what it is you want from—'

'I don't want anything,' she interrupted. 'But if this thing can be finished by me accepting everything, then I will.' End of subject, her tight voice intimated. 'They will be back tomorrow with their proposed settlements,' she predicted. 'I'll sign and we will catch our flight home.'

Never to return again, she vowed as she left the poor lawyer standing there looking both puzzled and frustrated. He'd been looking forward to a good fight. He'd had a taste of it and liked it; she'd recognised that in the Petronades boardroom today.

As she stepped outside, the full heat of the sun beat down upon her head. She paused for a moment to get her bearings before deciding to revisit some of her old haunts that did not remind her of Leandros. There were plenty of them, she mused cynically, as she flopped her sunglasses down over her eyes then walked off down the street. While Leandros had played the busy tycoon during her year here in Athens, she had learned to amuse herself by getting to know the city from her own perspective rather than the one her privileged Greek in-laws preferred.

Leandros had just managed to park his car when he saw Isobel step into the street. About to climb out of the vehicle, he paused to watch as she stood for a moment frowning fiercely at everything before she reached up to pull her sunglasses over her eyes, then walked off.

Where was she going? he mused grimly. Why wasn't she sitting in her room sobbing her heart out—as he'd expected her to be?

A stupid notion, he then decided when he took in what she was wearing. It was what he had used to call her battle-dress. When the hair went up in a pony-tail and her camera swung from her shoulder, and those kinds of clothes came out of the closet, his aggravating wife was making a determined bid for escape. How many times had he watched the back of that fine, slender figure disappear into the distance without so much as a word to say where she was going or why she was going there?

His jaw clenched because he knew *why* she had used to disappear like this. It had usually occurred after a row, after she'd asked him for something and he'd snapped at her because he'd been too busy to listen properly, and thought the request petty in the extreme. Guilty conscience raked its sharp claws across his heart. He'd been hell to live with, he recognised that now. He'd done nothing but pick and gripe and shut her up with more satisfying methods. And had never seen how lonely she'd been as she had walked away.

Climbing out of his sleek red Ferrari, he paused long enough to remove his jacket and tie then lock them in the boot. Then he intended to go after her.

But Leandros remembered the lover, and stopped as a whole new set of emotions gripped. Was he still in the hotel? Had she just come from him? Was he receiving the same walk-away treatment because he hadn't listened to what she had been trying to say? Had they rowed about the disaster this morning's meeting had turned into? Had she told the lover that she'd almost made love with her husband on the boardroom table before she walked away? Had *they* made love just now, in there, in that shabby hotel that suited clandestine relationships?

His mind knew how to torment him, he noted, as he slammed the car boot shut.

Where was his mother-in-law while all of this was going on? Was she lying on her sickbed with no idea that her daughter was romping with the body-builder in the next room? Maybe he should go and talk to Silvia. Maybe he should tackle the lover while Isobel was out of the way.

But his mother-in-law was a dish best eaten cold, he recalled with a rueful half-grin at the memory of her blunt tongue. And he wasn't cold right now, he was hot with jealousy and a desire to beat someone to a pulp.

Isobel disappeared around a corner; the decision about whom he was going to tackle first was made there and then. To hell with everyone else, he thought. This was between him and his wife.

It was good to walk. It was good to feel the tension leave her body the deeper she became lost in the tourist crowds. Isobel caught the metro into Piraeus, drank a can of Coke as she walked along the harbour, pausing now and again to snap photos of the local fishermen and their brightly painted boats. She even found her old sense of fun returning when they tossed pithy comments at her, which she returned with a warm grasp of Greek that made them grin in shocked surprise. Most people hated the busy port of Piraeus but she'd always loved it for its rich and varied tapestry of life.

An hour later she had walked to Zea Marina where the private yachts were berthed and ended up getting out of the heat of the sun in Mikrolimano beneath the awning of one of her favourite restaurants that edged the pretty crescent-shaped waterfront. She couldn't eat. It seemed that her stomach was still plagued by a knot of tension even if the rest of her felt much more at peace. But she was content to sit there sipping the rich black Greek coffee while taking in the spectacular views across the Saronic Gulf to the scatter of tiny islands glinting in the sun.

Eventually Vassilou, the restaurant owner, came out to greet her with a warm cry of delight and a welcoming kiss to both cheeks. It was that time of the day when Athens was at its quietest because most people with any sense were taking a siesta. The restaurant had very few customers and Vassilou came to sit beside her with his coffee while he tested her Greek.

It seemed crazy now, that she'd learned the language down here with the real people of Athens and not up there in the rarefied air on Lykavittos Hill, or Kolonáki, where the wealthy Athenians lived in their luxury villas. No one up there had thought it worth coaching her in the Greek language. They spoke perfect English so where was the need?

The need was sitting right here beside her with his thick thatch of silver hair and craggy brown face and his gentle, caring eyes. Not many minutes later they were joined by a retired sea captain, who began telling her some of his old sea yarns. Soon the chairs at her small table had doubled along with the circle of men. The restaurant owner's son brought coffee for them all and sat down himself.

Isobel was relaxed; she was content to sit and be entertained by these warm-hearted people. Despite her nightmare marriage to Leandros, she'd loved Athens—*this* Athens—and she'd missed it when she returned to London.

Suddenly she sensed someone come to stand behind her chair. Assuming it was another local, drawn to the little coffee-drinking group, she didn't think to glance round. She simply continued to sit there on a rickety chair with her coffee-cup cradled between her fingers and her smile one of wicked amusement while she listened—until a hand settled on her shoulder.

His touch caused a jolt of instant recognition. Her body froze and she lost her smile. The old sea captain's voice trailed into silence, and as each set of eyes rose to look at Leandros she had to watch the warmth die.

Not into frozen shock, she noted, but into looks of respect, the kind men gave to another when they recognised a superior man come down into their midst.

They also understood the gentle claim of possession when they saw it. These shrewd men of Greece understood the light, *'Kalimera,'* when it was spoken with the smoothness of silk. 'I understand now why my wife goes missing,' Leandros drawled lazily. 'She has other suitors with whom she prefers to spend the siesta hours.'

The words were spoken in Greek with the aim to compliment, and Isobel was not surprised when the grins reappeared. Men were always first and foremost men, after all. She sat forward to put down her coffee-cup, though ostensibly the movement was supposed to dislodge his hand. It didn't happen; the long brown fingers merely shifted to curve her nape then he bent and she felt the warmth of his breath brush her jawbone just before the brush of his kiss on her cheek followed suit.

He must know that her expression did not welcome him, but he was trusting her not to reject him here in view of all of these interested eyes. And, oddly, she didn't. Which troubled and confused her as she watched the sudden genial shift of bodies and listened to the light banter that involved excuses as the others left the lovers to themselves while they made a mass chair-scraping exodus to another table.

It took only seconds for her to know she'd been deserted. The reason for that desertion chose one of the vacated chairs and sat down. He didn't look at her immediately but frowned slightly as he gazed into the distance with his mouth pressed into a sombre line and the length of his eyelashes hiding his thoughts. He had lost his jacket and tie, she noticed, and the top two buttons to his shirt had been tugged free. He looked different here in the humid weight of natural sunlight, less the hard-headed business tycoon and more the handsome golden-skinned man she had first fallen in love with.

Her heart gave an anxious little flutter. She converted the sensation into a sigh. 'How did you know where to find me?' she asked then added sardonically, 'Still having me watched, Leandros? How quaint.'

The sarcasm made his dark head turn. Their eyes connected, the flutter dropped to her abdomen and she sank back in her chair in an effort to stop herself from being caught in the swirling depths of what those dark eyes could do to her if she let them.

'You speak and understand my language,' he said quietly.

It was not what she had been expecting him to say. But she hid her surprise behind a slight smile. 'What's the matter?' she mocked. 'Did you think your little wife too stupid to learn a bit of Greek?'

'I have never thought you stupid.'

Her answering shrug dismissed his denial. 'Inept and uninterested, then,' which added up to the same thing.

He didn't answer. He was studying her so intently that in the end she shifted tensely and found herself answering the dark question she could see burning in his eyes. 'I have always had a natural aptitude for languages,' she explained. 'And this...' her hand gave a gesture to encompass Piraeus in general '...was my classroom three years ago, where I learned Greek from the kind of people you've just scared off in your polite but esoteric way.'

'Esoteric,' he repeated. 'You little hypocrite,' he denounced. 'I have yet to meet a more esoteric person than you, Isobel, and that is the truth. You lived right here in Athens as my wife for a year. You slept in my bed and ate at my table and circulated on a daily basis amongst my family and friends. Yet not once can I recall you ever mentioning your trips down here to your *classroom* or revealing to any one of those people who should have been important to you that you could understand them when they spoke in Greek.'

'Oh, but I heard so many interesting titbits I would never have otherwise, if they'd known I understood,' she drawled lightly.

'Like what?'

Light altered to hard cynicism. 'Like how much they disliked me and how deeply they wished poor Leandros would come to his senses and see the little hussy off.'

'You didn't want them to like you,' he denounced that also. And his eyes threw back the cynical glint. 'You made no attempt to integrate with anyone who mattered to me. You just got on with your own secret life, picking and choosing those people you condescended to like and holding in contempt those that you did not. If that isn't bloody esoteric then I misunderstand the word.'

'No, you just have a very selective memory,' she replied. 'Because I don't recall a moment when any of those people you mention cared enough to show an interest in anything I said or did.'

'Most of them were afraid of you.'

She laughed, that was so ridiculous. His expression hardened. The anger of this morning's confrontation had gone, she noticed, but what had taken its place was worse somehow. It was a mood with no name, she mused, that hovered somewhere between contempt and dismay. 'You slayed them with your fierce British independence,' he continued grimly. 'You sliced them up with your quick, sharp tongue. You mocked their conservative beliefs and attitudes and refused to make any concessions for the differences between your cultures and theirs. And you did it all from a lofty stance of stubborn superiority that only collapsed when you were in my bed and wrapped in my arms.'

Isobel just sat there and stared as each accusation was lanced at her. Did he really see her as he'd just described her? Did he truly believe everything he'd just said?

'No wonder our marriage barely lasted a year,' she murmured in shaken response to it all. 'You thought no better of me than they did!'

'I loved you,' he stated harshly.

'In that bed you just mentioned,' she agreed in an acid-tipped barb. 'Out of it? It's no darn wonder I came looking for my own world down here where I belonged!'

'I was about to add that unfortunately love is not always blind.' He got in his own sharp dig. 'I watched you cling to your desire to shock everyone. I watched you take on all-comers with the fierce flash of your eyes. But do you know what made all of that rather sad, Isobel? You were no more comfortable with your defiant stance than anyone else was.'

He was right; she'd hated every minute of it. Inside she had been miserable and frightened and terribly insecure. But if he thought that by telling her he knew all of this gave him some high moral stance over her then he was mistaken. Because all it did was prove how little he'd cared when he'd known and had done nothing to help make things easier for her!

Love? He didn't know the meaning of the word. She had loved. She had worshipped, adored and grown weaker with each small slight he'd paid to her, with his *I'm too busy for this* and *Can you not even attempt to take the hand of friendship offered to you?* What hand of friendship? Why had he always had something more important to do than to take some small notice of her? Hadn't he seen how unhappy she was? Had he even cared? Not that she could recall, unless the rows had taken place in their bed at night. Then he'd cared because it had messed with that other important thing in his life—his over-active desire for sex! If she'd sulked, he'd thrown deriding names at her. If she'd said no, he'd taught her how quickly no could be turned into a trembling, gasping yes!

'Talk, instead of sitting there just thinking it!' he rasped at her suddenly.

She looked at him, saw the glint of impatience, detected the pulsing desire to crawl inside her head. Well, too late, she thought bitterly. He should have tried crawling in there three years ago!

'What do you want, Leandros?' she demanded coldly. 'I presume you must have a specific reason for tracking me down—other than to slay my character, of course.'

'I was not trying to slay anything. I was attempting to...' He stopped, his mouth snapping shut over what he had been about to say. 'I wanted to apologise for this morning,' he said eventually.

'Apology accepted.' But as far as Isobel was concerned, that was it. He could go now and good riddance.

He surprised her with a short laugh, shook his dark head then relaxed into his chair. 'Bitch,' he murmured drily.

It was not meant to insult, and oddly she didn't try and turn the remark into one.

Maybe this was a good time for Vassilou to bring them both fresh cups of coffee. He smiled, murmured a few polite pass-the-time-of-day phrases to which Leandros replied. Then, as he was about to leave, he turned back to send Isobel a teasing look. 'You never mentioned your handsome husband to me. Shame on you, *pethi mou*,' he scolded. 'Now see what you have done to my son? His hopes are dashed!'

With that he walked away, leaving her alone to deal with Leandros's new expression. 'Never?' he quizzed.

'For what purpose?' She shrugged. 'Our relationship had no place here.'

'You mean I had no place here—other than to keep eager young waiters at bay, of course,' he added silkily.

Without thinking what she was about to do, Isobel lifted her left hand up with the intention of flashing her wedding ring, which to her made the statement he was looking for without the need of words.

Only the ring wasn't there. Tension sprang up, her rib-cage suddenly felt too tight. No ring, no marriage soon, she thought and tugged the hand back onto her lap as an unwanted lump of tears tried to clog up her throat. Leandros looked on with his eyes faintly narrowed and his expression perfectly blank.

'Vassilou was making a joke.' Impatiently she tried to cover up the error.

'I know it was a joke,' he answered quietly.

'Then why have you narrowed your eyes like that?' she flashed back.

'Because the young waiter in question has been unable to take his eyes from you since you sat down at this table.'

'You've been watching for that long, have you? What did you do, hide behind a pillar and take snapshots every time he smiled at me?'

'He smiled a lot.'

She sat forward, suddenly too tense to sit still. She was beginning to fizz inside again, beginning to want to throw things at this super-controlled, super-slick swine! 'Why don't you just go now that you've made your apology?' she snapped, and picked up her coffee-cup.

Those luxurious lashes of his lowered to the cup; he knew what was going through her head. She'd done it before and thrown things at him when he'd driven her to it. Punishment usually followed in the shape of a bed.

But not this time, because she was not going to give him any more excuses to jump on her, she vowed, and took a sip at her coffee. It was hot and she'd forgotten to put the sachet of sugar in that she found necessary when drinking the thick, dark brew the Greeks so liked.

'Where is the lover?'

'What…?' Her head came up, green eyes ablaze because she was at war.

With herself. With him. She didn't know any more what was going on inside. She wished he would go. She didn't want to look at him. She did not want to soak in the way his head and shoulders were in a shaft of sunlight that seeped in through a gap in the striped awning above. She didn't want to see strength in those smooth golden features, or the leashed power in those wide shoulders.

He was gorgeous. A big, dark Latin-hot lover, with a tightly packed body lurking beneath his white shirt that could turn her senses to quivering dust. She could see a hint of black hair curling over the gap where he'd undone the top few buttons of the shirt. She knew how those crisp, curling hairs covered a major part of his lean torso. His rich brown skin was gleaming in the golden sunlight, and the sheen of sweat at his throat beneath the tough jut of his chin was making the juices flow across her tongue.

He was a man whom you wanted taste. To touch all over. A man whom you wanted to touch you. His hands were elegant, strong, long-fingered and aware of what they could do for you. Even now as they rested at ease between the spread of his thighs they were making a statement about his masculinity that sent desire coursing through her blood. His mouth could kiss, his eyes could seduce, his arms could support you while you flailed in the wash of rolling ecstasy the rest of him could give to you.

In other words he was a dark, sensual lover and she suspected one did not need personal experience of that to know it. A few weeks spent on his yacht in Spain and Diantha Christophoros must know it by osmosis. He was not the kind of man to hold back from something he wanted—as *she* knew from experience.

'The blond hunk with the lazy smile,' he prompted. 'Where is he?'

She blinked again and lowered her eyes. Oh, the temptation, she mused, as she stared at her coffee. Oh, the desire to say what was hovering right on the end of her tongue. 'His name is Clive and he's a physiotherapist.' She managed to control the urge to draw verbal pictures of Clive left sleeping off an hour's wild sex.

But her heart was still hammering out the temptation. She heard Leandros utter a soft, mocking little laugh. 'That cost you,' he taunted softly. 'But you had the sense to weigh up the odds of my response.'

'How is Diantha?' she could not resist that one.

Touché, his grimacing nod reflected. 'I have changed my mind about the divorce,' he hit back without warning.

'Well, I haven't!' she responded.

'I was not aware that I gave you a choice.'

'I don't think you have much control over my choice, Leandros,' she drawled witheringly. 'Why have you changed your mind?'

'Simple.' He shrugged, and with a bold lack of conscience lifted his hands enough for her to see what he was talking about. Pure shock sent a whole tidal wave of sensations washing through her.

'You should be ashamed of yourself!' she gasped in stunned reaction as heat poured into her cheeks.

He grimaced as if he agreed. 'I cannot seem to help it. I have been like this since you walked into my boardroom today. So, no divorce,' he explained. 'And definitely no other lovers until I get this problem sorted out.'

The problem being her and his desire for her, Isobel realised with a choke and incredulous disbelief that this was even happening.

'You are so excitingly beautiful,' he murmured as if that justified everything.

'But a bitch,' she reminded him.

'I like the bitch. I always did. It is part of your attraction I find such an irresistible challenge. Like the warning-red hair and the defy-me green eyes and the sulky little mouth that threatens to bite when I step out of line.'

His eyes were dark on her, his tone serious, the fact that he had already stepped out of line all part of what was beginning to burn between them. 'Everything about you I find an outright irresistible challenge,' he continued in a smooth, calm tone that could have been describing the weather, not what turned him on. 'When you walked into my boardroom this morning wearing leather, of all things, and it is thirty degrees out here, it was a challenge. When you sat there spitting hatred at me I don't know how I remained in my chair as long as I did before I leapt. I surprised myself,' he confessed. 'Now you sit here in military-style trousers and a T-shirt with your hair stuck in that pony-tail and you challenge me to crack the tough-nut you are pretending to be.'

'It's no pretence. I am tough,' she declared.

'So am I. And you can leap on me and try scratching my eyes out if you want to, but what *I* want will be the end result.'

'You still haven't told me what you want!' Isobel sliced

back at him. 'I haven't the slightest idea where you think you are going with this!'

'I want you, right at this moment,' he answered without hesitation. 'I thought I had made that absolutely clear. I want to close my mouth around one of those tight button breasts I can see pushing against your tough-lady top and simply enjoy myself,' he informed her outrageously. 'Though I would not protest if you dropped to your knees, unzipped my trousers and enjoyed yourself by taking me into your mouth—only I don't think the setting is quite right for either fantasy.'

'I think you're right, and I've had enough of this.' She got to her feet. 'Go to hell with your fantasies, Leandros.' She turned to leave.

As he'd done once before today, he moved with a silent swiftness that gave her no room to react. His hand curled around her wrist and with the simplest tug he brought her toppling down onto his lap. Her stifled cry of surprise slithered through the humid air and had a table of interested witnesses turning their way.

To them it must look as if she'd dived on Leandros rather than been pulled there, she realised, even as his eyes told her what was coming next.

'Don't you dare,' she tried to say but it was already too late. His mouth crushed the refusal, then began offering an alternative to both his fantasies with the help of his tongue.

It lasted short seconds, yet still she was too lost to understand what was happening when he broke the kiss, then quite brutally sat her back on her own chair again. Dizzy and dazed, flushed and shaken, she watched as he climbed to his feet. For a horrible moment she thought it was him who was going to walk away now and leave her to the humiliating glances.

Was that why he'd come here, tracked her down like

this and said what he had just said, just to pay her back for the way she had walked out on him this morning?

His hand dipped into his trouser pocket then came out again. Something landed on the table with a metallic ping. Money. She began to feel as if she had walked into hell without realising it. Had he thrown money down on the table to pay for the pleasure of treating her like this?

Stinging eyes dropped to stare and took long seconds to comprehend what it was they were staring at. Leandros sat down again. She couldn't breathe or think. Lifting her eyes, she just stared at him, her mouth still pulsing from the pressure of his kiss and her heart beating thickly in her throat.

Yes, Leandros thought with a grim lack of humour as he watched her flounder somewhere between this stunning moment and the kiss. You might be in shock, and you might be unable to believe I've just done what I did in broad daylight and in public view of anyone wanting to watch. But just keep watching this space, my beautiful wife, because I haven't even begun to shock you.

I should have done it years ago. I should have taken you by the scruff of your beautiful, stubborn, *tough*, slender neck and dragged you back into my life.

He was angry. Why was he angry? he asked himself. And knew the answer even before he asked the question. Every time he touched her she fell apart at the very seams with her need for him. Each time their eyes clashed he could see the hurt burning in hers because she was still so in love with him.

Which all added up to three empty, wasted years. Because if he'd faced her with their problems three years ago they would not be sitting here like two damned fools fighting old battles with new words. They would be in a bed somewhere enjoying each other in the traditional

Greek way. There could even have been another child to replace the one they'd lost, sleeping safely in a room close by.

And she would certainly not have let another man touch her! How could she do that anyway? he extended furiously.

'Put it back on,' he instructed, even though he knew she was incapable of doing anything right now.

'I don't—'

'Not your choice.' He was back to choices. 'While you are married to me you will wear my ring.'

'We are about to end our marriage,' she protested. 'What use is a wedding ring in a divorce?'

But even as she made that bitter statement he could see his kiss still clinging to the swollen fullness of her lips. The tip of her tongue could not resist making a sensual swipe across them in an effort to cool their pulsing heat. He mimicked the action with his own tongue, saw her breath shorten and her throat move convulsively. The old vibrations came to dance between them. The air became filled with the heady promise of sex. They had been here before, felt this before. Only then they had been eager to follow where those senses led them.

Now…?

'It means nothing any more,' she said and broke eye contact.

Was she referring to the ring or the sexual pull? he mused, and decided to deal with the former because the latter, he knew, was going to take care of itself in the not too distant future.

Leaning forward, he brought his forearms to rest on the top of the small wooden table, forcing a wary glance from her because she wasn't sure what was coming next. Once he had her gaze, he drew it down with the slow lowering of his lashes and let her watch as he worked his own ring free from his finger then placed it next to hers.

She was so very still he knew she understood what he was doing. The pulse in his throat began to pound. The two rings lay side by side in the sunlight, one large, one small, both an exact match to the other, with their gloss smooth outer surface and the inner circle marked by an inscription that said *My heart is here*.

How could he have forgotten that when he'd stood upon the deck of his yacht in San Estéban complacently making plans to finish their marriage? How could she have forgotten it when she tossed her ring back at him with such contempt earlier today? They had done this together. They had chosen these rings with their arms around each other, and hadn't cared how soft and stupidly romantic they must have appeared as they'd made the decision to have those words inscribed in those inner circles so they would always rest next to their skins!

'Now tell me it means nothing.' He laid down the rasping challenge as he watched her face grow pale. 'If you can bear to walk away and leave your ring on this table, then I will do the same. If you cannot bear to do that, put it back on your finger and we will talk about where we can go from here.'

Her tongue made a foray of her lips again. His teeth came together with a snap to stop him from moving close enough so his own tongue could follow in its wake. She was his, and the sooner she came to accept that the sooner they could work out their problems.

'The divorce—'

'The ring,' he prompted firmly.

She swallowed tensely. The mood began to sizzle with the threat of his challenge and her defiant need to get up and walk away.

But she could not do it. In the end and with a lightning flash of fury, she reached out, snatched her ring up and pushed it back onto her finger.

It went on easily because it belonged there. The next lightning bolt came his way. 'Now what? Do we go back to your office and talk divorce settlements again?'

Her waspish tone didn't hide anything. She was shaking all over and almost on the point of tears. She wanted him. She could not let him go. His ring was back where it belonged and he'd never felt so good about anything in a long time. Picking up his own ring, he slid it back where *it* belonged then sat back with a sigh.

'No,' he answered her question. 'We go somewhere more private where we can talk.'

Her look poured scorn all over that lying suggestion. She knew what he was intending. She was no fool. 'Try again, Leandros,' she murmured bitterly.

'Dinner, then. Tonight,' he came back. 'We will drive out of the city to that place you like in the mountains. Eat good food, drink champagne and reminisce over the good points in our marriage.'

His mockery flicked her temper to life, and he was pleased to see it happen because it was just the mood he was pushing for. Put Isobel in a rage and you had yourself an easy target, because as one guard fell the others quickly followed. So he relaxed back and waited for the sarcastic, What good points? to come slashing back at him. But what he actually got threw him completely.

'Sorry, my darling,' she drawled. 'But I already have a date tonight.'

Just like that it was his own temper deserted him. The lion inside him roared. He retaliated with swift and cruelly cutting incision. 'And there I was about to break my date with Diantha for you. But—no matter, you may bring your lover; we will make it a foursome. Maybe we will go home with different partners. Who knows?' He added a casual shrug. 'Maybe I will ache like this for Diantha and all my problems will be solved.'

He knew the moment he had shut his mouth that he had made some terrible tactical mistake. She'd gone so white he thought she might be going to faint away on him and her eyes stood out like two deep green pits of pain. She was standing up, not in anger, but on legs that did not wish to support her.

'I was referring to my mother,' she breathed, and this time she did walk away.

CHAPTER FOUR

YOU little liar, Isobel accused as she made good her escape. You meant what he thought you meant. What you didn't expect was the counter-thrust that punched another hole in your stupid heart!

But he wasn't coming after her, which probably meant they were back to square one, she thought heavily. Why am I here? Why am I letting him get to me like this? A three-year long separation should have dulled these wretched emotions out of existence!

The hotel was only a short walk away but by the time she arrived there she had the beginnings of a headache, so the last thing she needed was to walk into the hotel foyer and straight into a bored and weary reception party. Her mother, Clive and Lester Miles were all sitting on the few comfortable chairs the dingy foyer possessed. On a low table in front of them lay the remains of an indifferent-looking afternoon tea.

'Where have you been?' her mother demanded the moment she saw her. 'I've been worrying myself sick about you.'

'But I left you a message at Reception,' she said frowningly as she walked towards them.

'I got your message, Isobel,' her mother said impatiently. ' "*I've gone out for while,*" does not really cover a three-hour disappearance, does it? Having dragged me all the way to Athens, I did think you would have spared a little time to be with me.'

'But I thought...' she began, then changed her mind.

70

Her mother was right and attempting to shift responsibility on to the fact that Clive was supposed to be taking her out for the day wasn't good enough. Especially when it only took a glance at Clive to know he was wishing he hadn't invited himself along on this trip.

'I'm sorry,' she murmured, and bent to press a contrite kiss on her mother's cheek. It felt warm and she looked flushed. It occurred to her that they all looked flushed. Clive was sweating and Lester Miles had lost his suit jacket and tie and was fanning himself with an ancient-looking magazine.

It was then that she realised the air-conditioning wasn't working, and that it was as warm inside as it was out.

'It's broken,' Clive offered, noticing the way she'd glanced up at the air-conditioning vents set in the walls.

Broken, Isobel echoed wearily. No wonder her mother was cross. She had promised her faithfully that the hotel would be cool when she'd bullied her into coming here with her. With a deep breath she braced herself. 'Look,' she said. 'Why don't we go upstairs and all take a nice shower, then we can find somewhere to—?'

'We can't go upstairs, either.' It was Lester Miles that spoke this time. 'The lift has broken down as well.'

'As well?' she gasped. 'You have to be joking.'

'Nope.' It was Clive again. 'We are in the middle of a power cut, in case you haven't noticed. No lights, no air-conditioning and no lift,' he pointed out. 'Apparently it happens all the time.'

'So you tell me, Isobel,' Silvia said crossly, 'how a wheelchair-bound, feeble woman climbs four flights of stairs to get her much-needed cool shower?'

I don't know, she thought, and wondered what they would do if she plonked herself down on the floor and had a good weep? Nothing had gone according to plan from the moment she'd left here this morning. She wished she hadn't come to Athens. She wished she was still at home in rainy England, plodding away at her mundane photo-imaging job! She certainly wished she hadn't had to set eyes on Leandros again. He cut her up, he always had done. She lost her calm and steady sense of proportion whenever she was around him.

'You two men don't have to stay down here if you prefer to go and cool off in your rooms,' she murmured a trifle unsteadily. 'I'll see if Mum and I can find—'

'Trust me, Isobel,' Clive put in deridingly, 'we are sitting in the coolest place right now.'

'This place is a dump,' her mother added.

'I'm sorry,' her daughter apologised once again, realizing she *was* going to cry. She placed a hand to her aching head and tried to think. 'Just give me a few minutes—all of you—and I'll see if I can find us another hotel to—'

'Is there a problem here?' another, deeper voice inserted.

If it was possible, Isobel's spirits sank even lower as she turned with fatalistic slowness to face her nemesis. Leandros didn't look hot, she noticed. He didn't look anything but cool and smooth, suave and handsome and...

'What are you doing here?' It was her mother who asked the abrasive question.

'And good day to you, too, Silvia.' Leandros smiled, but his eyes remained fixed on Isobel's pale face. 'What's wrong?' he asked her gently.

Gentle did it. Her mouth began to wobble. The tears bulged in her eyes. 'I...' She tried to think but found that she couldn't. 'I...' She tried to speak again and couldn't even do that. It wasn't fair. *He* wasn't fair. He'd spun her round in circles until she didn't know what she was doing any more.

Leandros's hand came out in front of him. She saw he was holding her camera case out by its strap. She must have left it at Vassilou's restaurant. Maybe she'd left her courage there too. She reached out to take the camera back, missed the strap and found herself clutching at a solid male wrist instead. He didn't even hesitate, but just used her grip to propel her towards him and the next moment her face was pressed into his shoulder and she stayed there, not even caring who watched her sink so easily into the enemy.

One of his hands was gently cupping her nape; the other just as gently curved her waist. The camera was knocking against the back of her leg and her fingers were clutching at a piece of his shirt. He felt strong and reassuringly familiar and, though she did not want to feel it, there was not another place that she would rather be right now.

Someone was talking, someone was tutting. Someone else was also sobbing quietly and she knew it was her. He didn't speak. He just stood there and held her and listened.

Then she heard her mother snap, 'This it is all your fault, Leandros.'

'Quite,' he agreed, the single word vibrating in his deep chest and against Isobel's hot forehead. 'Mr Miles,' he spoke to her lawyer, 'would you do me a great favour and go over to that excuse for a hotel receptionist and tell him that Leandros Petronades wishes to speak to him?'

This blatant bit of name-dropping brought Isobel's face out of his chest. 'What are you going to do?' she asked.

'What you once told me I am good at,' he replied. 'Which is solving other people's problems.'

It was an old gripe, and it stiffened her spine to be reminded of it. 'I can do that for myself.'

'Stay where you are.' The hand at her waist slid up her back to keep her still. 'This is turning out to be one of the best days of my life, and you are not going to spoil it by turning back into the tough-lady I know so well.'

Her worst day, his best day. That just about said it all for Isobel.

As you would have expected, when Leandros threw his weight around, the hotel manager came out of his hide-away at great speed to begin apologising profusely in Greek. Leandros answered him in equally profuse but in-cisive Greek. The conversation was so swift and tight that Isobel couldn't follow it all. By the time the little man had hurried away again, Leandros was letting her ease away from him, and she then had to brace herself to face their audience.

Which made it the third time in one day she'd had to do it. Well, they said that bad things always come in threes, so maybe her luck was about to change, she thought hopefully as she glanced from hot face to hot face.

Her mother was staring at her as if she couldn't quite believe that her daughter had just wept all over her es-tranged husband. Lester Miles had put his jacket back on and was looking invigorated because he had been given something to do. Clive had come to his feet and was weighing up the competition. If he had any sense, it was all he would do, Isobel thought, then took in a deep breath and decided it was time to introduce him to Leandros.

'Clive, this is my husband Lean—'

'Silvia, *thoes*! You do not look well.' Cutting her off with a brusque exclamation, Leandros didn't even glance at Clive as he went to lean over her mother. 'This has been too much for you,' he murmured concernedly and took possession of one of her hands. 'You must accept my sin-cere apologies on behalf of Athens. You will give me five minutes only and I will make your life more comfortable, *ee pethera,* I promise you. If the manager is doing as I instructed then a car is on its way here as I speak. It will carry you with air-conditioned swiftness away from this miserable place.'

As Isobel watched, her stubborn, tough, I-hate-this-man mother melted before her very eyes. 'This hotel was all we could afford,' she told him miserably. 'Isobel wouldn't listen to sense. She wouldn't let you pay. And she wouldn't let me stay in my own home where at least I could make myself a cup of tea if I pleased.'

'Away to where?' Isobel cut in on this very enlightning conversation.

'To our home, of course,' Leandros replied. 'Isobel is a very stubborn woman, is she not?' he conspired with her mother. 'Which she gets from you, of course,' he added with a grin.

'I don't cut my nose off to spite my face,' Silvia pointed out.

'What do you mean, to your home?' Isobel gasped in outrage.

'*Our* home,' he corrected. 'I am relieved to hear that, *ee meetera*. It is such a beautiful nose. Perhaps between us we could persuade Isobel to leave her nose where it is?'

'You always were an inveterate charmer, Leandros,' Silvia huffed, but her cheeks were now flushed with pleasure rather than heat.

'Leandros. We are not going to stay at your house,' Isobel protested. 'The power cut will be over in a minute or so, then everything here will be back to normal!'

'And if it happens again when your mother is in her room?' he challenged. 'Is it worth risking her being trapped up there?'

'Just what I'd been about to say before you arrived.' Her wretched mother nodded.

Isobel threw herself into one of the chairs and gave up

the fight. 'What about Clive and Mr Miles?' she tossed into the melting pot of calamities that were befalling her today. 'They will have to come too.'

There was a sudden and stunningly electric silence. Then Leandros rasped, 'Your lover can sleep where the hell he likes, so long as it is not in my house.'

Her mother stared at him. Clive looked as if he had turned to stone. Lester Miles just watched it all avidly, like a man watching some gripping drama unfold.

Isobel's heart stopped dead. Oh, dear God, she groaned silently and covered her eyes and wished the world would swallow her up. Too late, she remembered that she'd left Leandros with the impression that she and Clive were lovers.

She couldn't take any more. She stood up. 'I'm going to my room,' she breathed shakily, and headed for the stairwell on legs that shook.

By the time she'd climbed up four flights and felt her way down a dingy inner corridor to her room, she was out of breath and so fed up that she headed straight for the telephone and got Reception to connect her with the airport. If she could get them home tonight then they were going, she decided grimly. Even if that meant travelling in the cargo hold!

No such luck. When a day like this began it didn't give up on turning one's life into a living hell. No seats were available on any flight out of Athens. She was stuck. Her mother was stuck.

'I'm sorry,' a voice said behind her. 'My coming here seems to have made a lot of problems for you.'

'Why did you come, Clive?' She swung round on him. 'I don't understand what you aimed to gain!'

He was standing propping up the doorway. 'I thought I might be of some use.' His shrug was rueful. 'Your mother agreed. It didn't occur to me that your husband would view my presence here with such suspicion.'

He didn't just suspect—he *knew* because she had told him! Oh, heck, she thought and sighed heavily. 'He's been having me watched,' she explained. 'When he heard that you were here he automatically assumed the worst.'

'It's nothing to do with him any more what I am to you,' Clive responded curtly. 'You came here to agree a divorce, not ask his permission to take a lover.'

Isobel released a thick laugh. 'Leandros is a very powerful, very arrogant, and very territorial man. The moment he heard about you, the divorce thing was dropped. Now I'm stuck with a man who has decided to work on his marriage rather than give me up to someone else.'

'That's primitive!'

'That's Leandros,' she replied, then sighed and sat down on the end of the bed.

'You don't have to go with him.'

No? I wish, she thought. 'He's already sweet-talked my mother with promises of air-conditioning and I can't even begin to list the rest of the luxury she is now looking forward to.'

'She doesn't even like the man.'

'Don't you believe that front she puts up,' she said heavily. 'My mother used to think he was the best thing that ever happened to me.' Until it all went wrong; then she'd wished him in hell.

Clive slouched further into the room. He was built like a cannon. All iron with a sunbed-bronzed sheen. The women adored him and flocked after him in droves. He worked at a fitness club. He spent hours patiently helping broken people to mend. He was *nice*!

'You came to Athens hoping I would need putting back

together again after meeting Leandros, didn't you?' she suddenly realized.

The painful part of it was that he didn't deny it. 'A man can hope.'

And a woman could dream. Her dream was downstairs right now, taking over her life. 'I'm sorry,' she murmured huskily.

He came to sit beside her on the bed. 'What are you going to do?' he asked.

Cry my eyes out? 'Give it a chance.' She shrugged.

On a sigh, Clive put a big arm around her and gave her a sympathetic hug. It was a nice arm, strong and secure and safe. But it was the wrong arm and the wrong man, though she wished it wasn't.

'Well, this is nice,' a very sardonic voice drawled.

Isobel felt her heart sink to her toes. Clive gave her shoulder a final squeeze then stood up. As he walked towards Leandros she could feel the hostility bouncing between the two of them. It conjured up images of dangerous cats again, only these were two big male predators considering testing each other's weight. They didn't speak. It was all part of the test to keep silent. Clive didn't stop walking and Leandros didn't move so their shoulders brushed in one of those see-you-later confrontations you expected from a pair of strutting thugs.

The moment Clive had gone, the bedroom door closed with a violent thud. Isobel got up and went over to the small chest of drawers and pulled open the top drawer for some reason she couldn't recall.

'My car has arrived,' Leandros informed her levelly. 'Lester Miles and my driver are taking your mother on ahead.'

'You should have gone with them.' It was not meant nicely.

'And leave you alone with the body-builder? You must think I am mad.'

'Clive is a friend, not my lover.' There, she'd told him. Now he could relax and return to the issue of divorce.

'Too late for that, *agape mou*,' he said deridingly. 'Though *ex*-lover, he most definitely is.'

'He is not my lover!' she swung on him furiously.

His black eyes flared. He moved like lightning, making her heart pound as he pushed his angry face up to her. 'Don't lie to me!' he barked at her. 'I am not a fool! I can count as well as you can!'

'Count?' She frowned. 'What are you talking about?'

His breath left his lips through clenched white teeth. If he touched her she had a feeling he would end up strangling her, he was in such a rage. But he didn't touch. He brought up his hand and placed four long fingers in front of her face. 'Four people. Three rooms,' he breathed severely. 'You tell me how that adds up! You tell me where the extra person sleeps!'

'Why, you...' The words got lost in a strangled gasp as it sank in what he was getting at. 'Clive did not share this room with me!' she denied shrilly. 'He didn't come as one of my party. He came under his own steam. Booked in under his own name—and his room is not even on this floor!'

He didn't believe her, she could see it as the savagery locked into his face. Without another word she slapped his hand away then stalked across to the wardrobe, threw open the doors then stood back. 'My room. My clothes!' she said furiously. 'My single bed!'

Her hand flicked out, sending his angry gaze lashing across the utilitarian plainness of a three-foot divan set in the shoebox this hotel called a single room.

'You know what you are, Leandros? You're the original

chauvinist pig! You dare to come up here showing me your
contempt for what you believe I've been doing with my
sordid little life—while you shack up with Diantha
Christophoros on your super-expensive bloody yacht!'

He spun to stare at her. 'What I said before about Di—'

'Talk about double standards,' she sliced over him. 'I
really ought to go and confront her now, just to even things
up a bit. Shall I do that, Leandros?' She threw out the
challenge. 'Shall I strut the strut? Get all territorial and
threaten to smack her in the face if she so much as looks
at my man? Maybe I should.' She sucked in a fiery breath,
breasts heaving, eyes flashing on the crest of a furious
wave. 'Maybe I should just do that and let the whole upper
echelons of this damn city know that Isobel, your scary
slut, is back!'

She was gasping for breath by the time she had finished.
He wasn't breathing at all and his face had gone pale. But
the eyes were alive with a dangerous glitter. 'Slut,' he
hissed out. 'You're no scary slut but just an angry woman
on the defensive!'

'Defending what?' she asked blankly.

'Your blond Adonis.'

At which point she knew she was in trouble. He didn't
believe her about Clive, and was coming towards her with
the slow tread of a man about to stake his claim on what
he believed belonged to him.

'Don't you dare,' she quavered, beginning to tremble as
his arm came up. His hand purposefully outstretched and
angled to take hold of her by the waist. If she backed up
she would be inside the wardrobe; if she stayed where she
was she was as good as dead meat for this predatory male.

'Andros—no,' she murmured shakily and tried a
squirming shift of her body in an attempt to evade what
was going to come.

His hand slid further around her waist and banded her to him. 'Say that again,' he gritted.

'Say what?' Too distracted by his closeness, she just looked blank.

'*Andros,*' he murmured in that low, deep, huskily sensual way that robbed her of her ability to breathe. Had she said his name like that? She couldn't remember. She hoped she hadn't because it gave too much away.

His other hand came up to coil around the thick silk lock of her pony-tail and began tugging with gentle relentlessness so he could gain access to the long column of her neck. She knew what was coming, her breath caught in her throat. If she let him put his tongue to that spot beneath her earlobe she was going to explode in a shower of electric delight.

'Say it,' he repeated, his eyes dark like molasses, his face locked in the taut mask of a man on the edge. His lips had parted, and were coming closer to her angled neck.

She released a stifled choke. '*Andros,*' she whispered.

His mouth diverted. It was so quick, so rewarding that she didn't stand a single chance. He claimed her mouth with devastating promise. He devoured it while she fought for breath. Her breasts heaved against his hard chest, her hips ground against the glorious power of his. Nothing went to waste, the kiss, touch, taste, scents, and even the sounds they made were collected in and used to enhance the whole experience.

It had always been like this. One second nothing, the next they were embroiled in a heady, sensuous feast. His fingers were in her hair. The next moment it was flowing over his hand and she quivered with pleasure because it always felt so very sexy when he set it free like this. Her T-shirt was easy; it disappeared without a trace. His shirt came next, revealing a torso that made her groan as she scraped her fingernails into the curling black mass of hair.

They kissed like maniacs; she nipped his lip, he bit back. Their tongues danced, their eyes locked together. She slid down his zip and covered him with the flat of her hand. He groaned something. He was hot and hard and out of control but then so was she. With one of his swift silent moves he picked her up and put her down on the divan bed then bent to rake the rest of her clothes down her legs.

'I'm going to eat you alive,' he said as he stripped himself naked. And he meant it. He began by bending his dark head and fastening on to one of her breasts. She squirmed with pleasure, her fingers clutching at his shoulders so she could pull him down next to her on the bed. He was magnificent, he was beautiful, his skin felt like oiled leather and she stroked and scored and kneaded it until he couldn't take any more and came to claim her mouth.

Every single inch of him was pumped up and hard with arousal. Every single inch of her was lost in a world of fine, hungry tremors that demanded to be quelled. They kissed, they touched, they rolled as a single sensual unit. When he reached between her legs, she cried out so keenly that he uttered a black oath and had to smother the sound with his mouth. The room shimmered in the golden light of the low afternoon sun. The heat was tremendous, their bodies bathed in sweat. His first plunge into her body brought forth another keening cry. He muffled this one with his hand. She turned her teeth on him, latching on to the side of his palm until he groaned in agonised pleasure, then pulled the hand away and finally buried his mouth in her neck.

Starbursts swirled in the steamy atmosphere. Her legs wrapped around his waist. With each thrust of his body she released another thickened cry and he groaned deep in his throat. It was a blistering, blinding coupling, incandescent and uncompromisingly indulgent in every sense. He brought her to the edge, then framed her face with his hands. His heart was pounding. His eyes were black, his beautiful mouth tight, his total commitment to what was about to happen holding his features drawn and tense.

The first flutters of orgasm took her breath away. He groaned, 'Oh, my God,' as her muscles rippled along the length of his shaft. His eyes closed, her eyes closed, and each flutter lengthened with each driving thrust until the whole experience became one long, tempestuous shower of sensation. It had always been like this for them; there wasn't a place where they could separate the sensuous storm at work inside each other.

Tenderness followed. It had to. They couldn't share something so deeply intimate and special then get up and walk away. Leandros rolled onto his back and took Isobel with him, curving her into his side with a possessive arm while he took deep breaths. Her cheek lay in the damp hollow of his shoulder; her arm lay heavy across his chest. She could feel the aftershocks at work inside him and turned her mouth to anoint him with a slow, moist kiss. It was one of those exquisite moments in time when nothing else mattered but what they were feeling for each other and through each other.

Then the lights flicked on. The small refrigerator in the corner began to whir. Muffled cheers sounded through the thin walls and reality returned with the electricity.

Leandros jerked into a sitting position then jackknifed off the bed. 'Tell me again that this bed is not big enough for two people,' he rasped and strode off to her tiny bathroom, slamming the door behind him in his wake.

He must be mad, he told himself as he turned on the poor excuse for a shower and attempted to wash the sweat from his flesh with tepid water that dribbled rather than sprayed.

Did he really want all of this back again? Did he want to feel so out of control all the time that he could barely think? She touched him and his skin was enlivened, she spat fury at him and it excited him out of all that was sane. She hated his family, she hated his lifestyle, she had learned his language but had not bothered to tell him so she could listen in like a sneaky spy on every conversation happening around her. She was already threatening to cause trouble and he would be a fool not to take her seriously.

He knew her. She was a witch and a hellion. Had he not reminded himself of these things only two weeks ago in Spain? Sluicing water down the flatness of his stomach, his hand brushed over the spot where she had laid her final kiss. Sensation quivered through him; hot and sweet, it caused a fresh eruption of flagrant passion to flow through his blood. Her barbs were not always sharp, he recognised grimly as he switched off the shower.

Grabbing one of the stiff hotel towels, he began to rub himself dry with it. It smelled of Isobel—her perfume was suddenly back on his skin and floating round his senses like a magic potion meant to keep him permanently bewitched. Did this dump of a hotel not even change the towels daily? Glancing around the tiny bathroom, he saw the signs of female occupation but no sign of a man's stamp anywhere.

No hint of a man's scent lay on the towels. Was she telling the truth? Ah, he would be a bigger fool to believe it, he told himself harshly. If the muscle-bound hulk did not know what it was like to fall apart in that woman's arms then he was no man, in his estimation.

Did he really want all of this back in his life?

It had been a day of madness, that was all; pure madness. He had seen and remembered and wanted and now had. It should be enough to let the rest of Isobel return to her other life so he could return to his.

But it wasn't, and he knew it the moment he stepped out of the bathroom with one of the towels wrapped round his hips. She was standing by the window in a blue towelling bathrobe, which looked familiar to him. Could it be the same one of his from his house in Athens that she used to pinch all the time because she liked to feel him close to her skin? Her hair lay down the back of it, her hands were lost in its cavernous pockets. He wanted to go over there and wind his arms around her but anger and frustration and outright damn *need* held him back from doing it.

Did he want to let her go again? Not in this lifetime. 'You can use the bathroom now,' he said as calmly as he could do and turned away from her.

'I will when you've gone,' she replied.

He was about to recover his scattered clothes when she said that but his movements froze on a sudden warning sting. 'In case you have forgotten,' he finished, bending to pick up his trousers, 'you are coming with me.'

'No, I'm not.'

His legs suddenly felt like lead beneath him. 'Of course you are,' he insisted. 'You cannot stay in this place, and your mother is…'

She turned to look at him then. His ribcage tightened in response. She looked so pale and fragile—ethereal, as if she could float away if the window were open.

'I would appreciate it if you could put my mother up for tonight,' she requested politely. 'You are right about this hotel; it isn't the place for her and I don't want to upset her further by moving her on again. But I'll stay here and collect her tomorrow in time for us to catch our flight home.'

'You come with me,' he insisted yet again and did not want to think about tomorrow.

But she shook her head. 'I think we've made enough mistakes for one day.'

'This is not a mistake.' Had he really just said that? While he had been locked away in the bathroom he had agreed with her. Now, when he could look at her again, he did not want it to be a mistake! 'We've just made love—'

'No,' she denied that, and what made it all the more frightening was that she did it so calmly. 'You've made your point.' A slight tilt of her head acknowledged his success at it. 'Two can lie in that narrow bed—I stand corrected. Now I would like you to leave.'

Leave, he repeated inwardly. She was dismissing him. 'So that the Adonis can get back in?'

Spark, he urged her silently. Say something like—Of course, he's waiting outside the door! Then I can retaliate swiftly. I can toss you back down on that blasted bed!

But she didn't say anything. She just turned and walked into the bathroom and left him standing there like a fool!

CHAPTER FIVE

LEANDROS turned to stare at the small hotel bedroom, with its scuffed grey marble flooring and the furniture that must have been there since the First World War. He stared at the bed with its coffee-coloured sheets covered with an orange spread made of cheap nylon, and thought of his own luxurious seven-foot bed set upon smooth white tiling and draped in cool mint-green silk over the finest white cotton sheets.

No effort was required to place Isobel's image on the mint-green coverlet, or to sit her cross-legged on the cool white floor while she sorted through a new set of photographs. Wherever he placed her in his bedroom, she created a glorious contrast to everything. He had missed that contrast in more ways than he had dared let himself know.

But he now had to ask himself if it was because he had missed her that he had gone to Spain and rarely returned to Athens for two years. Was it her ghost that had driven him out of his home and even now forced him to take a deep breath before he could walk back into it?

The sound of the shower being shut off had him moving out of his bleak stasis. By the time the bathroom door opened he knew what was going to happen next and that Isobel was going to have to accept it.

'What do you think you are doing?' Isobel came to a halt in surprised protest.

He was dressed and in the process of packing her suitcase. Beside the case, draped like a challenge on the bed, lay fresh underwear and the only dress she had brought with her to Greece.

'I believe that must be obvious,' he answered coolly.

'But I said…'

His glance flicked towards her. The way it slithered down her front made her heart give a shuddering thump. 'I recognise the robe,' he announced.

Without thought, her fingers went up to clutch the edges of her robe together across her throat. 'I…'

'You what?' he prompted, his dark eyebrows rising to challenge the guilty flush trying to mount her cheeks. 'You took it with you by mistake when you left me, then forgot to send it back to me? Or you stole it because you needed to take a part of me with you and have been hugging me next to your beautiful skin each time you have worn it since?'

'It's comfortable, that's all,' she snapped, shifting impatiently. 'If you want it back—'

'Yes, please.'

Without hesitation he walked towards her as if he was going to drag the stupid robe from her back! His dark eyes mocked the jerky step she took. They also saw the darkening swirl taking place in her eyes. He knew what that swirl meant. He knew everything about her.

Too much! she acknowledged helplessly as her senses began to clamour and he reached towards her with a hand. Prising her unwilling fingers free of the robe's collar, he then bent his dark head, buried his face in the soft towelling and inhaled.

'Wh-what are you doing?' she jerked out on a strangled breath.

'I am checking to see if you douse the robe with my aftershave,' he explained as he lifted his head. 'But no,' he sighed. 'It smells of you.' He took a step closer. 'And the promise of what awaits beneath.'

'I wish you would just stop this and leave,' she murmured crossly.

'Liar,' he drawled. 'What you want is for me to take the robe from you. You would love me to rip the thing from your body then throw you back on the bed and spend the next few minutes reminding you *why* I am still here!'

She was beginning to tremble. 'This is intimidation.'

'No,' he denied. 'It is a case of pandering to your preference for melodrama.' His fingers moved, releasing the towelling so he could brush a lazy fingertip across her pouting bottom lip. There was contempt in the small action but still her lip pulsed as the finger moved; it heated and quivered. 'You want me to *make* you surrender,' he said huskily. 'You would love me to use due force to make you come home with me so that you do not have to give up your precious stubbornness.'

Was he right? Yes, he was right, she conceded bleakly. Beneath the robe her body was already alive with anticipation, her breasts were tight, her abdomen making those soft, deep, pulsing movements that said fresh arousal was on its way.

With a toss of her head, she displaced his finger. 'It isn't home to me,' she denounced, utilising that stubbornness he spoke about. Then spoiled it all when her tongue slipped out to moisten the point where his finger had lingered.

Dark lashes lowered over even darker eyes as he watched the revealing little gesture. The power of his sexuality had never been a question for any woman who could witness that look. He was a dark golden figure with a dark, honeyed, sensual promise attached to everything he did.

'But it will be,' he assured, dragging her attention back

to the argument. 'Just as soon as you take off that robe and put on the clothes I have laid out for you, then we will drive *home*, together, as husbands and wives do—and find the nearest bed to finish what we have started here.'

With that, he turned and walked back to the suitcase, leaving her standing there having to deal with a sense of quivering frustration, which converted itself into a spitting cat. 'Will Diantha be joining us for a cosy little three-some?' she asked tartly. 'Or is this the point where I call up Clive and invite him along just in case we need the extra…?'

Her tongue cleaved itself to the roof of her mouth when he looked at her. Like the swinging gauge on a barometer, his mood had turned from tauntingly sexual to a cold contempt.

'There is no Diantha. There is no Adonis,' he clipped out with thin incision. 'This will be the last time either name will be mentioned in the context of our marriage again. Our marriage has just been re-consummated in this bed,' he added tightly. 'Here in Greece men still hold some authority over their women. Don't force me to impress upon you what that means, Isobel.'

He would, too, she realised as she stood staring at him while her mind absorbed his coldly angry expression. His willingness to be ruthless if she forced him into it was scoring lines of grim certainty into the lean cast of his face. Maybe she paled; she was certainly taken aback by his manner. They'd had many fights in their short-lived, highly volatile marriage, but she could not remember another time when he had used an outright threat.

Frissons sparked from one set of eyes to the other. Her fingers jerked up to clutch the robe again, closing the soft towelling across the pulse working in her throat. He watched it happen while he waited for a response from her. She saw a hard man, a tough man—much tougher than he had been three years ago. It was as if those years had taught him how to hone his strengths and use them to his own advantage. Four years ago he had been coming to terms with the knowledge that he no longer had a father to check every decision he made before it was put into action. Aristotle had been dead for only six months when Leandros and Isobel married. Leandros had been living with the stress of having to walk in a highly revered man's shoes. Advisors had hung around him like circling vultures, vying for a position of power in the new order of things that would eventually emerge from the melting pot of chaos into which his father's sudden death had thrown the Petronades empire. Leandros had lived in a permanent preoccupied state in which small things irritated the hell out of him because the big things totally obsessed his mind.

She had been a small thing. She had been a nagging irritant that he did not need during this dangerous cross-over period of his life. Oh, he had loved her to begin with. During that two-week sojourn in London, when most of the vultures had been left behind in Athens, he had been able to cast off his cloak of responsibility and become a carefree young man again for a while. So they met, fell in love, almost drowned in their happiness. Then they had come here to Athens, and he'd donned his heavy cloak again and become a stranger to her.

She hadn't understood then. She had been too young—only twenty-two herself. She had been too demanding, selfish and possessive and resentful of everything he placed higher on his list of priorities than her. Understanding had come slowly during the years they'd been separated, though the resentments had remained and hurts he'd inflicted upon her had refused to heal.

But she was now realising that Leandros had changed also. The circling vultures were no longer in evidence. The stress-packed frown of constant decision-making no longer creased his brow. He had grown into his father's shoes—had maybe even outgrown them to become a man who answered to no one, and was even prepared to be ruthless to get his own way.

'Why?' she breathed shakily. 'Why have you changed your mind about me?'

He did not even attempt to misunderstand the question. He knew they were back to divorce. 'I still want you,' he said. 'I thought that was obvious. All you need to do now is accept that you still want me and we can move on without all of this tedious arguing.'

'And if we make each other miserable again?'

He turned abruptly as if the question annoyed him. 'We will deal with that if or when it happens. Now, can we finish up here? Your mother's possessions still need to be packed and I would like to get away from here before the next power cut hits.'

He wasn't joking, she realised only half a second later, when there was a click, the lights went out and the fridge shuddered to a protesting halt. Problem solved, she mused bleakly. Stubborn desire to keep fighting him appeased.

Without another word she collected her clothes and returned to the bathroom, where it was pitch-black because there was no natural source of light in there. By the time she had fumbled into her clothes and knocked different joints against hard ceramic, she was more than ready to leave this hotel. Coming out of the bathroom, she found Leandros waiting for her by the open outer door.

'We are getting out of here while there is still enough light left to get down the stairs,' he said impatiently.

'But the bags—'

'The hotel will finish it and send your things on,' he announced with an arrogance that had always been there.

Before she knew it she was feeling her way down the dim corridor with her hand trapped securely in his.

'The city is being hit by lightning strikes due to a pay dispute,' he explained as they made it to the stairwell. 'The strikers are working on the principle that, because it is high season here in Athens, if they hit the tourist areas the government will sit up and take more notice, so the main residential areas are being left alone.'

'For how long, do you think?' She was feeling her way down the first flights of stairs while Leandros walked a few steps ahead of her.

'That depends on who is the most stubborn,' he replied, and turned his dark head to offer his first wide white grin. He was talking about them, she realised, not the strikers or the government.

Opening her mouth to make some tart reply, she missed her footing and let out a frightened gasp as she almost toppled. But he was right there to catch her. His hands closed around her slender waist and her body was suddenly crushed against his. Her stifled expression of fright brushed across his face and, on a soft oath, he trapped her up against the wall then lifted her up until their faces were level.

'I want you back in my life, my home and in my bed,' he declared with deep, dark, husky ferocity. 'I don't want us to fight or keep hurting each other. I want us to be how we used to be before life got in the way. I want it *all* back, *agape*. Every sweet, tight, glorious sensation that tells me that you are my woman. And I want to hear you say that you feel the same way about me.'

With her body crushed between the wall and the wonderful hardness of his body, and their eyes so close it was impossible not to see that he meant every passionate word, offering him anything but the truth seemed utterly futile. 'Yes,' she whispered. 'I want the same.'

In many ways it was a frighteningly naked moment. In other ways it was a relief. The truth was now out in the open and the only thing being held back were those three little words that would make exposure complete.

His dark eyes flared with the knowledge of that. She held her breath and refused to be the first one to say the words. 'Ruthless little witch,' he muttered thickly then his mouth found hers.

They actually shared, on that dim stairwell, the most honest kiss they had ever exchanged. It contained emotion, real emotion, the kind that rattled at the heart and dug its roots deep into that place where the soul lay hidden— along with those three small words.

When they were disturbed by the sound of someone else coming down the stairs, neither came out of the kiss breathing well. When Leandros levered his body away from her, he did so with a reluctance Isobel shared. She couldn't look at him, she was too busy trying to deal with the inner spread of those greedy roots of that oh-so-fickle thing called hope, that said yes, I want to take a risk on this. It is what's been missing for all of these years.

They continued their way downstairs into the foyer. The profusely apologetic manager listened as Leandros issued curt instructions about the packing of possessions and where to send them. The other man tried not to appear curious as to why the wife of Leandros Petronades had been staying in his hotel in the first place.

'He thinks we are very odd,' Isobel remarked as they stepped outside into a pink-glow sunlight.

'I feel very odd,' he came back drily—and caught hold of her hand.

Life suddenly felt so wonderful. Leandros's car was parked fifty feet away. It was low and sleek and statement-red and so much the car for a man of his ilk. Opening the door to the Ferrari, he guided her into the passenger seat, watched her coil her long legs inside, watched her tug her skirt down, filled her up with all of those sweet, tight sensations he had been talking about on the stairs, then closed the door to stride round the long bonnet and take the seat at her side.

The air was electric. He turned the key in the ignition and brought the car alive on a low, growling roar. The nerve-ends between her thighs flicked in tingling response to the car's deep vibration. The man, the car—it was like being bombarded by testosterone from every possible source, she thought breathlessly.

Did he know she was feeling like this?

Yes, he knew it. She could see his own tension in the way his long fingers gripped the squat gear stick, and the way his sensual mouth was parted and his breathing was tense as he looked over his shoulder so he could reverse the car in the few inches available to him to ease them out of the tight parking place. There was a hint of red striking along his cheekbones; his eyes glittered with that strange light that told her she was sitting beside a sexually aroused male. When he turned frontward again, she was showered with static. He changed gear, turned the steering wheel with one of those smooth fingertip flourishes that said the man controlled the car and not the other way around.

With a blaring of car horns he eased them out into the stream of traffic. The low sun shone on her face. She reached up to pull down the sun-visor and found her hand caught by another. The way he lifted it to his mouth and kissed the centre of her palm stifled her ability to breathe for long seconds. As he drove them through the busy streets of Athens, they communicated with their senses. He refused to release her hand, so when it became necessary to change gear it was her hand that felt the machine's power via the gear stick, with his hand holding it there.

It was exciting. She could feel sparks of excitement shooting from him, could feel the needle-sharp pinpricks attacking her flesh. Beneath the dress her breasts felt tight and heavy, between her thighs it was as if they were already having sex.

When they were forced to stop at a set of traffic lights he turned to look at her. His eyes filtered over her face then down her front. The dress was short, but not as short as she had used to wear three years ago, when glances like this used to be accompanied by a frown. This time her thighs were modestly covered but still he made her feel as if she were sitting there naked. The inner tingling turned into a pulsing. She tried pressing her thighs together in an effort to contain what was happening to her. His eyes flicked up, caught the anxiety in her eyes, the way she was biting down on her soft lower lip.

'Stop it,' she protested on a strangled choke of breathless laughter.

'Why?' was his devastatingly simplistic reply.

Because I am going to embarrass myself if you don't stop, she thought helplessly, but suspected that he already knew that.

The lights changed and he turned his glance back to the road again. She managed to win her hand back and tried to ignore what was passing between them. But the bright white of his shirt taunted her with what hid beneath it. If she reached out and touched him she knew she would feel the tension of muscles held under fierce control, and she could see a telling pulse beating in his strong brown neck that made her heart thump madly with the urge to lean across the gap separating them and lay her moist tongue against his throat. The way he moved his shoulder said he'd picked up on the thought and was responding to it.

They began to climb out of the city where the mishmash of buildings gave way to greener suburbs and breathtaking views over Athens to the sunkissed waters of the Saronic Gulf. Eventually they began to pass by the larger properties, set in their own extensive grounds and built to emulate classical Greece. Leandros's mother had a house here, though further up the hill. They drove past the Herakleides estate, where his Uncle Theron lived with his granddaughter Eve, who had been perhaps the only person in the family Isobel felt at ease with.

But then Eve was of a similar age and she was also half-English. She might be the very spoiled and the worshipped grandchild of a staunchly Greek man but she had always determinedly hung on to her British roots.

'Eve is married now,' Leandros broke their silence to inform her.

'Married?' Isobel turned disbelieving eyes on him. The girl she remembered had been a beautiful blonde-haired, blue-eyed handful of a creature who'd constantly foiled her grandfather's attempts to sell her into bondage—as Eve had called it.

'It's a long story,' he smiled, 'and one I think you will enjoy more if I let Eve tell it to you.'

The smile was rueful and turned her heart over because it reminded her of when he'd used to offer her sexily rueful smiles all the time. Rueful smiles which said, I want you. Rueful smiles which said, I know you want me but we will have to wait.

This smile was rueful because he knew what she was thinking about his precocious cousin Eve. But Isobel didn't smile back because she was remembering that, for all her staunch Englishness, Eve was adored by her Greek family. It was Eve's mother who had never made the grade. As Eve had once told her, 'They accept me because I do have their blood in my veins, even if I like to annoy them all by pretending I don't. But my poor mother was looked upon with suspicion from the moment she came here with my father. Thankfully, we spent the first ten years of my life living in London so the family didn't have a chance to put any spanners in the works of my parents' marriage. When they died and I was sent here to live with Grandpa they felt sorry for me so I got the sympathy vote. But that doesn't mean I don't know what they can be like, Isobel. Just do me one great favour and don't let them win.'

But they had won in the end. And, although Isobel remembered that Eve's grandfather had always been pleasant to her, she had never trusted his genial manner. Because like his much younger sister, Thea Petronades—Leandros's mother—Theron had no real wish to see the Herakleides blood-line further diluted with yet more English blood.

'Who did she marry?' she asked Leandros. 'Someone from a great Greek family no doubt?'

'Eve, meet Theron's expectations?' He grinned. 'No, she married a tough British bulldog called Ethan Hayes. And I don't think he is ever going to recover from the shock.'

'Who, Theron?' she prompted with just enough cynicism to wipe the grin from his face.

'No, Ethan Hayes,' he corrected. 'And your prejudice is showing, *agape*.'

Her prejudice? She opened her mouth to protest about that accusation then closed it again when she realised that he was right. She was prejudiced against these people. The knowledge did not sit comfortably as he turned the red car in through a pair of gates that led to the house that had once been her home.

This house was not as grand as the Herakleides mansion—or the Petronades mansion further up the hill. Leandros's mother still occupied the other home along with the rest of the Petronades family. But still, this building had its own proud sense of presence and made no secret of the fact that it belonged to a very wealthy man. Leandros had bought it just after they were married in an attempt to give them some private space of their own in which to work out the problems they were already having by then. His mother had taken offence, said it was not the Greek way, and if Isobel could not live with the family then maybe it should be Thea and the rest of the family who should move out, since the Petronades home had belonged to Leandros since his father's death.

Problems—there'd been problems whichever way she'd turned back then, Isobel recalled with a small sigh. Leandros heard the sigh, pulled the car to a stop in front of the neat entrance, switched off the engine then turned to look at her.

Her expression was sad again, the flush of sensual awareness wiped clean away. He wanted to sigh too, but with anger. Was the sight of their home so abhorrent to her? He glanced at the house and recalled when he'd bought it as a desperate measure in the hope that it would give them some time and space to seal up the cracks that had appeared in their relationship. He'd even got a friend in to refurbish the whole house before he'd brought Isobel down here to surprise her with his new purchase.

But all he had achieved was yet another layer of discontentment. For she'd walked in, looked around and basically that was all she could do. He had realised too late that to have the house decorated and furnished ready for occupation by some taste-sensitive interior designer had been yet another slight to Isobel's ability to turn this house into a home for them.

Home being an awkward word here, he acknowledged bleakly. For it had never become one—just a different venue for their rows without the extra pairs of ears listening in. He had still worked too many hours than were fair to her. She had still walked away from him down this sunny driveway each morning without a backward glance to see if he cared when he watched her go.

It was her one firm statement, he realised now, as they sat here remembering their own history of events. Because his working day had begun later than Isobel had been used to in England, she had left him each morning with her best friend, her camera, when really she knew he would much rather have been lingering over breakfast with her—or lingering somewhere else. If he came home at siesta time, she had rarely ever been here to greet him. After he'd burned the midnight oil working, she had been very firmly asleep when he'd eventually joined her in the bed. If he'd woken her she'd snapped at him and the whole circus act had begun all over again. Stubbornness was her most besetting sin but his had been gross insensitivity to the lonely and inadequate person she had become.

Strange, he mused now, how he did not move back into the big family house after she had left him for good. Strange how he'd preferred to leave Athens completely, having continued alone here for almost a year.

Hoping that she would return? he asked himself as he climbed out of the car and walked around its long, shiny red bonnet to help her alight.

Long legs swivelled out into the sunlight, cased in sheer silk; he caught the briefest glimpse of lacy stocking tops before the dress slid back into place. Classically styled and an elegant blue, the dress was not dissimilar to the one Diantha had been wearing the day he'd made his decision to break his marriage link to Isobel. But as she took his hand to help her to rise upright, there was nothing else about this woman or the dress that reminded him of any of those thoughts he'd had back then. In fact he could not believe his own thick-skinned arrogance in believing he could prefer Diantha's calming serenity to this invigorating sting of constant awareness that Isobel never failed to make him feel.

She was beautiful, stunningly so. As she came to stand in front of him he watched the loose fall of her shining hair as it slid silk-like across her slender shoulders, the curving shape of her body moving with innate sensuality beneath her dress. The length of her legs would make a monk take a second look but, for him, they made certain muscles tighten because he could imagine them wrapped tightly around his waist.

He was just contemplating that such a position might not be a bad idea with which to make the transition from here into the dreaded house, when he noticed a familiar car parked beneath the shade of a tree. His brows came together on a snap of irritation. Drawing Isobel towards him, he made do with dropping a kiss to the top of her head as he closed the door to the Ferrari and wondered how he was going to explain this away.

There was no explanation, he accepted heavily. He was in deep trouble and the only thing to do was to get it over with.

CHAPTER SIX

WALKING towards the house took more courage than Isobel had envisaged. The moment Leandros swung the front door open her stomach dipped on a lurching roll of dismay. The late-afternoon heat gave way to air-conditioned coolness in the large hallway, with its white glossed banister following the graceful curve of the stairs to the landing above. The walls were still painted that soft blue-grey colour; the tiles beneath her feet were the same cool blue and grey. To the left and the right of her stood doors which led into reception rooms decorated with the same classy neutral blend of colours and the kind of furniture you only usually saw in glossy magazines.

This house had never felt like home to her but instead it was just a showcase for this man and a bone of contention to everyone else. She had been miserable here, lonely and so completely out of her depth that sometimes she'd used to feel as if she was shrinking until she was in danger of becoming lost for good.

A strange woman dressed in black appeared from the direction of the kitchens. She was middle-aged, most definitely Greek, and she offered Isobel a nervous smile.

'This is Allise, our housekeeper,' Leandros explained, then introduced Isobel to Allise as *my wife*.

Wondering what had happened to Agnes, the cold fish his mother had placed here as housekeeper, Isobel smiled and said, '*Hérete*, Allise. It's nice to meet you.'

'Welcome, *kiria*,' the housekeeper answered politely.

'Your guests await you on the terrace. I shall bring out the English tea for everyone—yes?'

It felt odd to Isobel to be referred to for this decision while Leandros stood beside her. Agnes used to look to Leandros for every decision, even those simple ones regarding pots of coffee or tea. 'Yes—thank you,' she replied in a voice that annoyed her with its telling little tremor.

'What happened to Agnes?' she asked as Allise hurried back to her kitchen.

'She left not long after you did,' he replied, and there was something in his clipped tone that suggested it had not been a friendly parting of the waves.

But this was not the time to go into domestic issues. Isobel had a bigger concern looming forever closer. It came in the shape of her mother, and how Silvia was going to take the news that, having watched her daughter go off this morning ready to end her marriage, Isobel was now agreed to trying again.

Indeed, the marriage had again been consummated, as Leandros had so brutally put it.

They took the direct route to the terrace, treading across cool tiling to a pair of French doors at the rear of the house that stood open to the soft sunlight. They didn't speak. Isobel was too uptight to talk and she could feel Leandros's tension as he walked beside her. Was he worried about her mother's reaction? she wondered, and allowed herself a small, wry smile, because if she were in his shoes she would be more worried about his own mother's response when she found out about them.

The first person Isobel saw was her mother, sitting on one of the comfortable blue-covered cane chairs, looking a bit happier than she had done the last time she'd seen her. Lester Miles was there too, but he was wearing a brooding frown and he jumped to his feet the moment he saw them step outside.

Her mother glanced around; a welcome smile lit her face. 'Oh, there you are,' she greeted brightly. 'We were just wondering where you'd both got to!'

The *we* didn't register as meaning anything special until someone else began to rise from the depths of another chair. She was small, she was neat, she was dark-haired and beautiful. Even as she turned to them, Isobel knew who it was she was about to come face to face with. She had met her just once during a hastily put-together dinner party meant to celebrate Leandros's surprise marriage. The dinner party had been a complete disaster, mainly because everyone was so very shocked at the news, none less than Diantha Christophoros.

'I've just been explaining to Diantha how kind it was of you to put us up here after our dreadful experience at that awful hotel, Leandros,' Isobel's mother was saying with all the innocence of someone who had no idea whom it was she was giving this information to.

Leandros allowed himself a silent oath, and decided that if lightning could strike Silvia dumb right now, he would lift his eyes in thanks to the heavens. As it was, even the older woman had to feel Isobel stiffen and see the faintly curious expression Diantha sent him that had a worryingly amused and conspiratorial gleam about it.

He tried to neutralise it with an easy smile. 'Diantha,' he greeted mildly. 'This is a surprise. I don't think I recall that you were expected here today.'

Wrong choice of words, he realised the moment that Isobel took a tense step away from him.

'I know, and I am sorry for intruding like this,' Diantha replied contritely. 'Allise should have warned me that you

had guests arriving unexpectedly, then I would not have
made myself quite so at home.'

'Oh, you've been a great help,' Silvia assured in her
innocence. Lester Miles was standing there looking dis-
tinctly ill at ease. 'We hope you don't mind, Leandros, but
with stairs being a problem for me Diantha has arranged
for your handyman to set up a bed in that nice little annexe
you have attached to the main house. I think I will be very
comfortable there until we catch our flight back to
London.'

'It was my pleasure, Mrs Cunningham.' Diantha smiled
a pleasant smile. 'I hope you will enjoy the rest of your
stay in Athens. Leandros,' she turned back to Leandros
without pause in her smooth, calm voice, 'I need a private
word with you before dinner this evening. Your mother—'

His mother. 'Later,' he interrupted, feeling very edgy
due to Isobel's silent stillness. What was more apparent
was the way Diantha was ignoring Isobel. Did she believe
she had a right to do that?

Had he allowed her to believe she had that right?

'Isobel, darling, you look very pale,' Silvia inserted.
'Are you feeling OK?'

No, Isobel was not OK, Leandros thought heavily. She
believed Diantha was his lover. She had believed Diantha
was the woman he had been about to put in her place. Her
chin was up and her eyes were glinting. It was payback
time for the way he had treated her Adonis and he did not
for one moment expect Isobel to behave any better than
he had done. But for all that he might deserve the payback,
Diantha was innocent in all of this. He could not afford
an ugly scene here, and turned urgently to face his statue
of a wife.

'Isobel...' he began huskily.

'Oh, you do look pale!' Diantha exclaimed gently. Then

she was smiling warmly as she walked forward with a hand outstretched towards Isobel, and Leandros was at a loss as to how to stop what he knew was about to take place. The air began to sing with taut expectancy; he felt the sensation attack his loins. 'I don't suppose you remember me, Isobel,' Diantha was saying pleasantly. 'But we met once, at…'

Isobel turned and walked back into the house, leaving the horrified gasps echoing behind her and the sound of Leandros's urgent apologies to his mistress ringing in her head!

Striding back down the hall with the heels of her shoes tapping out a war tattoo against hard ceramic, she opened a door that led to one of the smaller sitting rooms at the front of the house. She stepped inside the room and slammed the door shut.

'Get out of here,' she lanced at Leandros when he managed to locate her several seething minutes later. 'I have nothing to say to you, you adulterous rat!'

'Back on form, I see,' he drawled lazily.

She turned her back to him and continued to glare out of the window that looked out on the front of the house. Her arms were folded beneath her heaving breasts and she could actually feel the fires of hell leaping inside.

The door closed with a silken click. A shiver chased down the rigid length of her spine. He hadn't gone. She could feel him standing there trying to decide how best to tackle the fact that his wife had just come face to face with his mistress!

'You were very rude.' He began with a criticism.

Typical, she thought. Attack instead of defence. 'I learned from an expert.'

'I suppose you are referring to me?'

Got it in one, she thought tightly. 'I hate this house.'

'As you hate me?'

'Yes.' Why bother denying it? She hated him and she could not believe she had let him seduce her into coming back here. She had to have gone temporarily insane. The whole day had been one of utter insanity, from the moment she'd got into that cab this morning with Lester Miles!

She heard his sigh whisper across the room, then felt the smooth, steady vibration of his tread as he began to walk towards her, her fingers curled into two tight fists. Suddenly she was having to fight a blockage in her throat.

'As soon as my luggage arrives I'm leaving,' she muttered.

He came to a stop an arm's reach away; she could feel his presence like a dark shadow wrapping itself around her shivering frame. If he touches me I won't be responsible for my actions! she told herself shrilly. If he dares make excuses I'll—

'Is that why you're staring out of the window?' He issued a soft, deriding laugh. 'It is just like you, Isobel, to cut and run in the face of trouble. I now have this great image of you walking up that driveway dragging your suitcase behind you. It looks so pathetically familiar that it makes me want to weep!'

His angry sigh hissed; she spun around to face him. She was shocked by how pale he looked in the deepening glow of the evening light. His clothes had lost their normal pristine smoothness and he needed a shave. Sinister was the word that leapt up to describe him. Sinister and frustrated and so angry it was pulsing out of every weary pore.

How could a man change so much in a few short minutes? It was this house, she decided. This hateful, horrible house. And that image of her that he had just conjured up was dragging on her chest and tugging out the tears.

'Don't you dare compare this with my life here before!' she cried.

'*Our* life!' he barked at her. 'Whatever happened here before happened to *both* of us! But we are not discussing the past.' His hand flicked out in an irritable gesture. 'We are discussing here and now, and your propensity to run instead of facing what threatens to hurt you!'

'I am not hurt, I'm angry!' she insisted. His mouth took on a deriding twist. The flames burning inside her leapt to her eyes.

'Diantha—'

'Is so comfortable here she instructs your staff on what to do!'

'She is a natural organiser,' he sighed out heavily.

He was daring to stand here defending his mistress? 'Just what you need, then,' she said. 'Because I can't even organise a pot of tea!'

He laughed; it was impossible not to. Isobel turned away again and managed to break free.

'I did not marry you for your organisational skills,' he murmured huskily.

Sex; they were back to the sex, she noted furiously.

'I married you because you are gorgeous and sexy and keeping my hands off you is like having an itch I cannot scratch.'

Her spine began to tingle because she knew her husband and he had just issued fair warning that he was going to touch.

'Get your mistress to scratch the itch,' she suggested.

'Diantha is not my mistress.'

Scornful disbelief shot from her throat. 'Liar,' she said.

The light touch of his fingers feathered her bare arms. Excitement shivered across every nerve-end. He was standing so close now her body was clenching in defence against that sensational first brush with his thighs.

'She is a close family friend, that is all.'

Isobel's second huff of scorn sent those fingers up to gently touch her hair. She was suddenly bathed in a shower of bright static.

'This conversation is developing a distinct echo to it,' he then tagged on ruefully.

He was comparing it with their row about Clive. 'The difference here being that I *know* about Diantha. You just jumped to conclusions about Clive because you have that kind of mind.'

'He was *raw* with desire for you,' he growled close to her earlobe.

'Whereas she only wants you for the prestige of your money and your exalted name.'

His low laugh of appreciation brought his lips into contact with her skin, at which point she was about to turn, deciding that braving eye contact had to be easier to deal with than the assault Leandros was waging on other parts. But a noise beyond the window caught her attention. Leandros straightened when he heard it too, and both of them watched a van come trundling down the drive bearing the name of the Apollo Hotel on its side.

Her luggage was about to arrive. Her heart began to thud. It was decision time. Did she stay or did she go?

'I stayed, *agape mou*,' Leandros said gruffly. 'Despite the suspicions I still have about you and the Adonis, I am still here and fighting for what I want. Don't you think it is about time that you stood still and fought for what you want?'

Fight the mistress? She did turn and look at him. 'Are you challenging me to go and throw her out of this house?'

A sleek black eyebrow arched in counter-challenge. 'Will it make you feel better about her if you did?'

No, it wouldn't, she thought bleakly, because throwing Diantha out of this house would not be to throw her far enough. 'You hurt her once before by marrying me in her place. Are you really prepared to do that to her again, Leandros?'

'I don't know what you're talking about.' He frowned.

Isobel's sigh of irritation was smothered by the sound of the van coming to a shuddering stop outside the window. 'I do know about your old romance with her,' she told him heavily. 'If an ordinary high-street lawyer like Lester Miles can find out about your present relationship, then we are talking about a serious breach of Greek family ethics here, of which—'

'Just a minute,' he cut in, and the frown had darkened. 'Back up a little, if you please. What old romance am I being accused of having with Diantha?'

He was going to make her spell it out. 'The way your sister Chloe told it, you virtually jilted Diantha at the altar when you married me.'

'Chloe?'

'Yes, Chloe,' she confirmed and could not stand still a moment longer looking into the clever face of confusion. Stepping round him, she put some distance between them. Outside a van door gave a rattling slam. 'Within days of you producing me as your wife, Diantha's family were shipping her off to Washington, DC and away from the humiliation you caused her.'

He was following her tense movements with increasingly glowering eyes. 'And my sister Chloe told you this?' he demanded. Her shrug confirmed it. 'When—when did she relay these things to you?'

'Does it matter?'

'Yes, it matters!' he snapped. 'Because it is not true! Nor is this—rumour, which seems to be everyone else's property but mine, that I am about to divorce you to marry her! I do not know who began it, and I can positively tell you that Diantha has received no encouragement from me—at either time—to believe that I have a marriage between her and me in mind!'

'Are you saying you have never considered marrying her?' Her challenge was etched in disbelief. But when he released a hard sigh then turned *his* back to *her*, Isobel knew the truth.

'Stop playing with people, Leandros,' she snapped and walked towards the door.

'I am likely to do a lot more than play, Isobel, if you try to walk through that door before we have finished this line of discussion.'

A threat. She stopped. Somewhere beyond these four sizzling walls a doorbell gave a couple of rings. She turned to face him. He was furious, she saw. Well, so was she! 'It was one thing playing the interloper here four years ago but to hell with you if you think I am going to go through all of that again!'

Her eyes were bright, her mouth trembling. If he dared to, he would go over there and...

And what? Leandros asked himself angrily. Force her to believe that which he could not deny outright? 'I had no such relationship with any other woman before I met you,' he announced thinly. 'Diantha did not leave Athens nursing a heart broken by me,' though he could tell who had broken her heart. 'Before Diantha arrived on my yacht in Spain as a hurried substitute for Chloe, who was needed here by my mother, I had not set eyes upon her in four years. During the two weeks Diantha stayed with me, we neither kissed nor slept together and very rarely touched.

But I did find her easy company to be with,' he admitted. 'And on an act of pure arrogance I made a decision that maybe—just maybe—she would eventually make a wife for me. The one I had did not, by that time, have much use for me, after all!'

'So it's my fault that you gave everyone the impression that you were divorcing me to marry her. Is that what you're saying?'

'No,' he sighed. 'I am saying that I was arrogant, but only within my own head!'

'But she uses this house as if she belongs here because *she* is arrogant.' If Isobel fizzed any more she was going to pop like a champagne cork, Leandros noted frustratedly.

'She is a friend—that is all,' he gritted. 'A *good* friend, who has been helping me out by liaising between myself and my mother, who is a neurotic mess because of Nikos's big wedding next week!'

'Liaising,' she scoffed. 'That's a good one, Leandros. Now I'm hearing repeated lies!'

Oh, to hell with it, he thought, and began striding towards her. Someone rattled the handle on the door. It flew inwards, forcing Isobel to leap out of its way and bringing him to a stop almost within reach of his aggravating target.

Isobel's mother appeared in the opening, propelling herself in her wheelchair. She looked cross—everyone was cross!

'Would you like to explain to me, young lady,' Silvia flicked sternly at her daughter, 'what happened to the good manners I taught you? How could you be so rude as to turn your back on that nice Miss Christophoros and walk away? I have just had to spend the last half an hour covering up for you!'

'That *nice* Miss Christophoros you have been happily *liaising* with happens to be *my* husband's mistress!'

Silvia's furious daughter replied, and, having silenced her
mother, she then stalked away, hair flying like a warning
flag, long legs carrying her out of the room and—

Leandros went to go after her...to stop her from leaving,
then halted again when he saw her take to the stairs. A
grin appeared. The minx might want to take his head off
right now, but she was not going to leave him.

'What was she talking about?' Silvia demanded.

'She's jealous,' he murmured. 'She does not know what
she's saying.'

'It sounded pretty clear-cut to me,' Silvia countered. 'Is
that woman your current mistress?'

Current? He pondered on the word while he listened for
that old familiar sound of a door slamming somewhere.
Rear bedroom, not his, he calculated when, as predicted,
the sound came.

Diantha, he noticed, had gone from being *that nice Miss
Christophoros* to *that woman*. Silvia was nothing if not
loyal to her own. Which brought forth another thought.
'Where is Diantha?' he asked sharply.

'She left just as the luggage arrived. Didn't you hear
her car pull away?'

No, he had been too busy fighting with Silvia's witch
of a daughter. 'Silvia,' he said, coming to a decision, 'you
may not like what I am about to tell you, but I suggest
you come to terms with it. Isobel and I are not getting a
divorce,' he announced. 'We are, in fact, very much a re-
united couple.'

He had to give it to his mother-in-law—she was not
slow on the uptake. Her eyes went round. 'In just half a
day?'

He smiled; it was impossible not to. 'It took less than
half a day the first time we met,' he admitted candidly.

'That was before you broke Isobel's heart and sent her

home to me in little pieces,' Silvia said brutally. Eyes as fierce and contrarily vulnerable as her daughter's glared at him. 'I won't let you do it to her again.'

'I have no intention,' he assured. 'But I warn you again, Silvia,' he then added seriously, 'Isobel is still my wife and is staying that way.'

Isobel's mother studied his grimly determined expression. 'I think you should try telling her that,' she advised eventually.

'Oh, she knows it.' His eyes narrowed. 'She is afraid of what it is going to mean, that's all.'

'And the mistress?'

He mocked the question with a grimace. 'Is a mere friend.' The sooner certain other people recognised that the quicker he could settle down to convincing Isobel. 'Where is the lawyer?' he then asked thoughtfully.

'Still on the terrace looking slightly poleaxed by high-society living.'

Nodding, Leandros went to walk past her then paused and instead bent his dark head to place a kiss on her cheek. Her skin felt as smooth as her beautiful daughter's. But then Silvia was still a very attractive woman, even sitting here in this wheelchair. She had her daughter's eyes and beautiful mouth, and, though her hair might not be as red as Isobel's any more, it was still luxuriously silken.

'I am happy to see you back here again, *ee peteria*,' he told her huskily. 'But I am not happy to see you confined to this thing.'

'It won't be forever,' Silvia replied firmly. 'I am getting stronger by the day and don't usually spend so much time sitting here.'

'Would it be too much for you to explain to me what happened?'

Ten minutes later he was going to find Lester Miles,

with his head so filled with his new insight into Isobel and Silvia's last few years while they'd fought Silvia's battle together, that he didn't notice Isobel sitting on the top stair, where she'd listened in on the whole illuminating conversation.

When he'd gone she came down the stairs and brushed her mother's cheek with a silent salutation. She'd had no idea how tough her mother had found the last two years until she heard her confiding in Leandros.

'Come on,' she said softly. 'Let's go and check out your new accommodation.' And, taking charge of the wheelchair, she turned it round to face the hallway.

'You OK?' Silvia asked.

'Yes,' Isobel answered.

'You still love him don't you?'

'Yes,' she answered again; there was really nothing more either of them could add to it.

Together they checked over everything and found nothing to complain about. The rooms had used to be a fully self-contained study added on by a previous owner of the house who was a writer and liked his own space when he was working, so most of the necessary facilities had been built into the annexe. When the designers moved in they'd converted the whole thing into a state-of-the-art office for Leandros. But he'd rarely used it, preferring to use the conventional study in the main part of the house. Isobel had taken it over to use as a photo studio, where she'd developed her photographs and played around with them via the computer sitting in the corner on its state-of-the-art workstation.

With Diantha's famed organisational skills, a bed had been added along with a couple of armchairs and a huge TV set. Reluctant though Isobel was to admit it, the place looked great.

'I'll want for nothing here,' her mother announced with satisfaction. Even her luggage had been carefully unpacked and put away.

Now she must go and check on their other guest, she realised. 'Where's Lester Miles?' she asked her mother.

'Ask Leandros,' she suggested. 'He went looking for him a few minutes ago.'

But Lester Miles was being driven away from the house even as Isobel went to search him out. 'What have you done with my lawyer?' she demanded when she met Leandros in the hall.

'He's just left.'

Her very expressive eyes began to flash. 'Don't tell me you've sent him back to rough it at the Apollo!'

'No.' His mouth twitched. 'He had to go back to England with some urgency. My driver is taking him to the airport.'

'He won't get a flight,' Isobel stated confidently.

'Oh?' he murmured curiously. 'Why not?'

'Because all the flights to London are full—I already checked,' she drawled.

'How enterprising,' he commended. 'Were you hoping to escape *before* we made it to the bed or afterwards?'

Refusing to answer that, she turned and started up the stairs. Leandros arrived at her side.

'I am flying your lawyer home—along with the Adonis. There,' he smiled. 'Am I not a graciously accommodating man?'

Refusing to rise to that bit of baiting, she kept her gaze fixed directly ahead.

'Where are we going?' he enquired lightly.

She was on her way to find her own luggage; where he was going did not interest her one little bit.

He smiled at her again. She wanted to hit him. 'Is your mother comfortable?' he enquired.

'Perfectly, thank you,' she answered primly.

The sound of low laughter curled her insides up. They arrived on the upper landing, where six doors led to elegant bedroom suites. Isobel made for one door while Leandros made for another. With their hands on the door handles they paused to glance at each other, Isobel with the light of defiance in her eyes, because the room she was about to enter was not the one they'd used to share. Leandros simply smiled—again.

'Dinner,' he said, 'eight-thirty,' and disappeared from view, leaving her standing there seething with anger and a sense of frustration because, by refusing to comment on the fact that she was clearly not intending to share a bedroom, he had managed to grab the higher ground.

Dinner was a confusing affair. Silvia was tired and had decided to eat in her room then watch a video film before going to bed. Isobel came down, wearing the same dress—since it was her only dress. Though she had taken a shower, pinned up her hair and added some light make-up.

Leandros on the other hand was wearing full formal dinner dress. He looked handsome and dashing and her heart turned over. 'A bit over the top for an informal meal in, isn't it?' she remarked caustically.

'I have to go out later,' he explained. 'My mother is expecting me, and, since I have been strictly unavailable to anyone today, either I turn up or she will come here to find out what I am playing at.'

Isobel wished she knew what he was playing at. There were undercurrents at work here that made her feel out of control. Yet she didn't know why, because it wasn't as if she hadn't known about the dinner tonight. Diantha had mentioned it, being so efficient. What she had expected was that Leandros would make some concession for once in his important existence and have remained here with her.

Which was telling her what? she asked herself. She didn't like the answer that came back at her, and that revolved around dear Diantha and his preference for where he would rather be!

They walked into the smaller of the two dining rooms that the house had to offer, like two strangers on their first date. Leandros politely held out a chair for her. Allise, she saw, had pulled out all the stops for this cosy dinner for two and the table had been dressed with the best china and candles flickered softly instead of electric lights.

She sat down. Leandros helped her settle her chair. By the time he'd moved away without so much as touching her even by accident, she was feeling so incensed she felt she was living within her own personal battle zone.

He sat down opposite. Candlelight flickered over lean, dark features completely stripped of his thoughts. He was beautiful. It wasn't fair. The black of his jacket and the white of his shirt and the slender bow-tie gave sophistication a whole new slant. He reached for a napkin, shook it out then took a bottle of champagne out of its bucket of ice. The napkin was folded around the bottle. Long brown fingers deftly eased out the cork. It popped softly but did not dare to explode—not for this man who had learned how to open a bottle of champagne in his crib. Frothy gold liquid arrived in the crystal goblet in front of her without him so much as spilling a drop. He filled his own glass. She considered picking up hers and tossing the contents at him.

But the suspicion that he was already expecting her to do that held her hands tightly clenched on her lap. If he didn't say something to ease this tension, she was going to be the one to explode…like the champagne cork should have done.

'You can come with me, if you want.'

She sat there staring at him, unable to believe he had just said that—and as casually as he had done!

'Thank you,' she said coolly. 'But I am watching a film with my mother.'

His grimace said—fair enough. He picked up his fizzing crystal goblet and tipped it in a suave toast to her. 'Welcome home,' he said, then drank.

If Allise hadn't arrived with the food at that point, maybe—just maybe—Isobel would have reacted. But wars like this required nerves of steel and she had them, she told herself.

They ate in near silence. When she couldn't push her food around her plate any longer, Isobel drank some of the champagne, which instantly rushed to her head. Her mouth suddenly felt numb and slightly quivery. She put the goblet down. Leandros refilled it. Allise arrived with the second course. When the last course arrived, Isobel refused the delicious-looking honey-soaked pudding and asked for a cup of black coffee instead. She'd drunk two glasses of champagne like a woman with a death wish because she knew as well as Leandros knew that she had no head for the stuff.

When the dreadful meal was finally over, she got up on legs that weren't quite steady. Leandros didn't get up but lazed back in his chair, studying her without expression.

'Goodnight, then,' she said.

He gave a nod in acknowledgement. She walked out of the room. She suffered watching the film with her mother out of grim cussedness, then escaped to her self-allotted bedroom, got ready for bed, crawled beneath the crisp white sheets, pulled them over her head and cried her eyes out.

He was with her, she was sure of it. He was standing in some quiet corner of his mother's house, gently explaining the new situation. Would she beg, would she cry? Would he surrender to the liquid appeal in her dark eyes and stay with her tonight instead of coming home?

She drifted into sleep, only to be consumed by visions she did not want to see. It wasn't fair. She hated him. He was tying her in emotional knots just like the last time. A pair of arms scooped her off the bed and jolted her out of sleep.

CHAPTER SEVEN

'GET off me, you two-timing brute!' she spat at him.

'Well, that isn't very nice,' he drawled.

'Where do you think you are taking me?'

'You did not really think that I was going to let you sleep in any other bed than our own, did you? Foolish Isobel,' he mocked as he lifted up a knee then swung her down onto another bed.

The knee stayed where it was, the rest of him straightened so he could remove his robe, his eyes glinted dark promises down at her, and because she was too busy trying to cover her dignity by tugging her ridden nightshirt over the shadowy cluster of golden curls at her thighs she missed her only chance to escape. He came down beside her in a long, lithe stretch of male determination. One hand slid beneath the fall of her hair while the other made a gliding stroke down her side from breast to slender thigh. Then it came back up, bringing her nightshirt with it.

He stripped it from her with an ease that left her gasping. She aimed a clenched fist at him, he caught it in his own hand, then his mouth was coming down to cover her mouth. She groaned out some kind of protest but it wasn't enough to bring this to a halt. It was dark, it was warm and, as he subdued her, her senses were already beginning to fly. Seconds later she was lost in the hungry, driving intensity of the kiss.

Her fingers unclenched out of his grip on them, lifted then buried themselves in his hair. The kiss deepened. She could feel his heart pounding, felt the thick saturation of his laboured breath. Her body, her limbs, every sinew moved and stretched on wave after wave of desperate delight. He dragged his mouth away and looked down at her, no smile, no mockery, just heart-stunningly serious desire.

'Did you go to her?' she whispered painfully.

'No,' he replied.

'Was she there?'

His eyes darkened. 'Yes.'

Her fingers tugged at his hair until he winced. 'Did you speak to her—touch her?'

'No,' he grated. 'I had no reason to.'

The black ferocity of his gaze insisted that she had to believe that. Her mouth slackened into a wretched quiver. 'I imagined all sorts,' she shakily confessed to him.

'I am with the only woman who has *ever* done this for me,' he answered harshly. 'Why would I lust after less?'

'Three years, Leandros,' she reminded him painfully. 'Three years can make a man accept less.'

'Were you unfaithful?' He threw the pain right back at her.

'No—never.'

'Then why are we talking about this?'

They didn't talk any more, not after his mouth claimed hers again and his hands claimed the rest of her with a grim, dark, fierce concentration that robbed her of the will to do anything but feel with every single sense she possessed.

She was possessed, Isobel decided later, when she lay curled in the secure circle of his arms. Her cheek rested in the hollow of his shoulder, her fingers were toying with the whorls of hair on his chest. There wasn't another place she would rather be, but knowing it made her feel so very vulnerable. She didn't think she was any better equipped now than she had been three years ago to deal with what loving a man like Leandros meant.

She released a small sigh. The sigh aggravated the muscles controlling Leandros's steady heartbeat. She might be lying here in his arms but he knew she had problems with it. Did he take a leap of faith and force those problems out into the open so they could attempt to sort them out?

He trapped his own sigh before it happened. He didn't want to talk. His eyes were heavy, his body replete and content. Her hair lay spread across his shoulder, her soft breathing caressed his chest and the darkness soothed him towards sleep.

She moved just enough to place a kiss on his warm skin, then followed it up with another pensive sigh. Contentment flew out of the window. He moved onto his side and flipped her onto her back then came to lean over her with his head supported by his hand.

'What?' she said and she looked decidedly wary.

'Why the melancholy sighs?' he demanded.

'They were not melancholy.'

He arched an eyebrow to mock that little lie. She lowered dusky eyelashes until they brushed against skin like porcelain. Her mouth looked small and cute when he knew that the last thing you could ever call Isobel was *cute*.

'I have this urge to stand you up against the nearest wall and shine a bright light in your eyes,' he murmured drily. 'We have just made love. You cried out in my arms and clung to me as if I was the only thing stopping you from falling off the edge of the earth. You told me you loved me—'

'I did not!' The desire to deny that brought her lashes upwards.

'You thought it, then,' he amended with a shrug meant to convey a sublime indifference to semantics. Then he reached out to gently comb her hair from her face, and was suddenly serious. 'We need to talk, *agape mou,* about why we parted.'

Without the gentleness she might not have caught on to what he was actually daring to broach here. But he saw the light in her eyes change, saw them flood with horror then with tears. 'No,' she said, then was leaping out of the bed and racing from the room.

By the time he had grabbed his robe and gone after her she was standing in the other bedroom, huddled inside the blue robe. His chest ached at the sight of her, at the sight of that robe that said so many things about the real Isobel, like the look of pure anguish whitening her face.

'Will you stop running?' he ground at her. 'Just stop running from this,' he repeated almost pleadingly. 'If we do not face the past together, how are we supposed to move on?'

Isobel stood and shook and remembered why she hated him. If she could take back the last mad day then she would. Her heart hurt, her throat hurt; just seeing him standing there looking as if he was experiencing the same things made her want to wound him as he had once almost fatally wounded her. How could she have forgotten what he had done to her? How could she have lain in his arms and let herself ignore the kind of man she knew him to be?

'You didn't want our baby,' she breathed. 'Is that facing it?'

He winced as if the tip of a whip had just lashed him. 'That is not true…'

'Yes, it is,' she insisted. 'By the time I was pregnant I don't think you even wanted me!'

'No…' He denied that.

'I was the irritation you just didn't need, and you made

sure I knew it.' But he was right; she could not run from this! It had to be faced before they made the same mistakes a second time and turned lust into love, which then turned into regret filled with frustration and bitterness. 'You married me when you didn't need to, we both knew that— you'd already enjoyed what was on offer after all! You lifted me out of working-class drudgery into wealth and luxury beyond compare then expected me to show eternal gratitude. But how did I pay you back for this generosity and goodness? I refused to conform. I refused to smile weakly and say ''Yes, thank you, Mama,'' when your mother lectured me on how I should behave.'

'She was attempting to advise you.'

'She was cold and critical and so dismayed by me that I don't know how she managed to stay in the same room with me half the time!'

'So you played up to that criticism, is that it?' he bit out. 'Or should I say you played down to it just for the hell of watching her squirm?'

'I stayed *away* from it!' she corrected. 'Or didn't you notice?' She was aching and throbbing as it all came rushing back. 'I went out and found my own kind of people.' Her hand stretched out to encompass the view of Athens lying beyond the window.

'Like Vassilou.'

'Did your mouth flatten like that in distaste, Leandros?' she challenged the expression on his grim face. 'If you can't see the difference between *''Do you really need to wear those terrible trousers, Isobel?''* and *''Ah, Kyria, you look so cool and fresh today!''* well, I certainly can. Or—*some babies are ill-judged and ill-timed, Isobel.*'Her eyes began to sting. She swallowed thickly. 'Words like that when spoken by the mother of your husband rarely shore up an ailing marriage. They help to shatter it.'

'My mother could not have said such a thing to you,' he denied, but he'd gone pale. He knew she was telling the truth. 'She would not be so—'

'Cruel?' she finished for him when the word became glued to his tight upper lip. '*"Maybe it was for the best."*' Hoarsely she quoted his own choice of words back at him. '*"We were not ready for this."*'

He swung his back to her and walked over to stare out of the window. The desire to leap on that back and pummel it to the ground sang in her blood. If she shook any more fiercely she would have to sit down. He had lifted the lid on black memories, and now she was standing here being consumed by them.

'I was ashamed of myself when I said that,' he uttered.

'Good,' she commended. 'I was ashamed of you too.' With that she walked over to the chest of drawers and withdrew a fresh nightshirt then went into the bathroom. She didn't shut the door because she was *not* running away this time. Not from this—not from anything *ever* again.

He came to stand in the doorway. With her back firmly to him she dropped the robe and replaced it with the clean nightshirt. 'You were inconsolable and I did not know how to cope with your grief,' he said huskily.

'No, you were busy and had to be pulled out of an important meeting,' she gave her own version of events. 'And if it wasn't bad enough that you didn't want me to get pregnant in the first place, you then found yourself having to deal with an hysterical woman who didn't appreciate '*"Maybe it is for the best."*'

'All right,' he rasped. 'So I did not want us to have a baby at that time!'

She swung round to look at his face as he dared to admit that! No wonder his skin looked grey!

'We were both too young. Our marriage was in a mess!

You were miserable; *I* was miserable! We had stopped communicating on any level—'

'Especially between the sheets.'

'Yes, between the bloody sheets!' he grated, and suddenly he was swinging away from the door and gripping her upper arms. 'I adored you. You fascinated me! You sparkled and sizzled and took on all-comers with a courage that took my breath away. When you were in my arms it was like holding something powerfully special. But our marriage had not had the time to grow beyond that all-consuming physical obsession before you were presenting me with a red stop light. I resented having to stop!'

'I didn't ask you to.'

'You did not need to.' His sigh took the anger out of him; dropping his hands, he moved away. 'You did not see how fragile you looked, as if you would shatter if I so much as touched you.'

He walked back into the bedroom. This time it was Isobel that followed him. 'Couldn't you have just told me that instead of turning cold on me?'

'Tell you that I was such a selfish swine that I did not want half a lover in my bed?' He released a self-derogatory laugh. 'Tell you that I did not want to share your body with anything?' An oath was thrust out from the cavernous depths of his chest. 'I despised myself. I did not know what was happening inside my own head! When you lost the baby I believed I had wished it to happen. I still believe that. My punishment was to lose you, and I was willing to take it. I was willing to take any punishment so long as I was not forced to face you with what I had done.'

'So you let me walk away.' She understood him now.

'You tied me in so many knots I was relieved to see you go.'

'And broke my heart all over again,' she said with painful honesty. 'Didn't it occur to you that I needed you to come for me?'

His shook his head; his shoulders were hunched, his gaze grimly fixed on his bare feet. 'I despised myself. It was easy, therefore, to convince myself that you despised me too.'

'I did.'

Silence fell. It came with a heavy thud. Isobel looked at the spacious bedroom with its cool floors and lavender walls and purple accessories, and wondered how silence could hurt so much.

'It wasn't your fault,' she murmured eventually. 'The baby, I mean,' she added, then had to swallow tears when he lifted his dark head to send her an agonisingly unprotected look. 'The statistics for losing a first baby in the first three months of pregnancy are high. It was simply bad luck.'

She tried a shrug to punctuate her absolute belief in that, but it didn't quite come off and she had to turn away in the end, wrapping her arms across her body and clutching at her shoulders with tense fingers that shook. A pair of arms arrived to cover her arms; long fingers threaded tensely with hers. It was so good to feel him hold her that she couldn't hold back the small sob.

'I had my own guilt to deal with,' she thickly confided. 'I felt I had failed in every way a woman could. I had to leave because I couldn't stand everyone's pitying expressions and the knowledge that they thought the loss of our baby more or less summed up our disaster of a marriage.'

He remained silent but his arms tightened, offering comfort instead of words. On a small whimper she broke the double arm-lock so she could turn and give back some comfort by placing her arms around his shoulders and pressing her face into the warm strength of his neck.

'Tomorrow we begin making a better job of this second chance we have given ourselves,' he ordained gruffly.

She nodded.

'We talk instead of fighting.'

She gave another nod.

'When people say things you do not like you tell me about it and I listen.'

She agreed with another nod.

He shifted his stance. 'Don't go too meek on me, *agape mou*,' he drawled lazily. 'It makes me nervous.'

'I'm not being meek,' she informed him softly. 'I'm just enjoying the feel of your voice vibrating against my cheek.'

With a growl, she was lifted up and kissed as punishment. The kiss led to other things, another room and a familiar bed. They slept in each other's arms and awoke still together, showered together and only separated when Isobel had to go back to the other bedroom to find something to wear.

They met up again on the terrace. The first cloud that blocked out her sunlight came when she saw Leandros was dressed for the office in a dark suit, blue shirt and dark tie. Handsome and dynamic he may look, but she needed him to stay here with her.

'For a few hours only,' he promised when he saw her expression, getting up to hold out a chair for her.

'It is reality, I suppose.' She smiled.

'And some unfortunate timing,' he added. 'I have been back in Athens for only a few weeks after a long stay abroad. Nikos's marriage is like a large juggernaught racing down a steep hill and taking everyone else along with it for the ride.'

Was he talking about his time in Spain as his long stay abroad? Isobel wondered. But didn't want to think about that right now when she was trying hard not to think of anything even vaguely contentious.

'So, when is the wedding?' she asked brightly.

'Next week.' He grimaced as he sat down again. 'In my father's stead I have been slotted into the role of host for the many pre-wedding dinners my mother has arranged, and also as to escort her to those that the Santorini family are having. Hence my having to leave you last night.' He paused to pour her a cup of coffee. 'Tonight I must do the same—unless I can talk you into coming with me?'

Body language was one hell of a way to communicate, Leandros mused as he watched her smile disappear and her eyes hide from him while she hunted for an acceptable excuse to refuse.

It came in the shape of Silvia Cunningham, who appeared on the terrace then. She was walking with the aid of a metal frame, and even to him it was a worthy diversion.

He stood up and smiled. 'What a delightful sight!' he exclaimed warmly. '*Ee pateria*, those beautiful legs look so much better when viewed upright.'

'Get away with you,' Silvia scolded, but her cheeks warmed with pleasure at the compliment. 'You know, I can't make up my mind if it is the fierce heat or the relentless sunshine, but I feel so much stronger today.'

Isobel got up to greet her mother with a kiss then pulled out a chair for her and waited patiently while Silvia eased herself into it. As he watched, Leandros saw the tender, loving care and attention Silvia's daughter paid to her comfort without making any kind of fuss.

He also noticed the look of relief on her face because their conversation had been interrupted. Stepping across the terrace to where the internal phone that gave a direct line to the kitchen sat, he ordered a pot of tea for Silvia then came to sit down again. He listened as mother and daughter discussed what kind of night Silvia had had while thoughts of his own began to form inside his head.

Allise arrived with the pot of tea. There was a small commotion as room was made on the table and an order for toast and orange juice was placed. Biding his time, he sipped at his coffee, watching narrowly as Isobel used every excuse she could so as not to look at him.

She was wearing the green trousers teamed with a white T-shirt today. The hair wasn't up in a pony-tail, which had to mean that she was not about to run. But, beautiful though she undoubtedly was, fierce and prickly and always ready for a fight, she was also a terrible coward. It had taken him a long time to realise that, he acknowledged, as he watched her bright hair gleam in the sunlight, her green eyes sparkle as they smiled at Silvia and her very kissable mouth curve around her coffee-cup.

He waited until both ladies had put their cups safely down on their saucers before he went for broke. 'Silvia,' he aimed his loaded bet directly at Isobel's weakest point, 'Isobel and I must attend a party tonight. We would be very honoured if you would accompany us.'

He had chosen his bet well, for he could remember Silvia before her accident. She might have spent her working hours stuck behind the window as a teller in a high-street bank but her social life had used to be full and fun.

'A party, you say?' Eyes so like her daughter's began to sparkle. 'Oh, what fun! And you really don't mind if I come along with you?'

From across the table, barbs began to impale him. He made eye contact with a brow-arching counter-challenge that gave no indication whatsoever to what was beginning to sizzle in his blood. This woman could excite him without trying to. She brought him alive.

'We didn't come to Athens equipped to attend parties,' Isobel reminded *both* of them.

Silvia's face dropped in disappointment. Isobel saw it happen and looked as if she had just whipped a sick cat.

'No problem,' he murmured smoothly. 'It is an oversight that can be remedied within the hour.'

'Of course!' Silvia exclaimed delightedly. 'We have time to shop, Isobel! It's about time we treated ourselves to something new!'

I hate you, the other pair of eyes informed him. The sulky mouth simply looked more kissable.

'Whose party is it?'

With the smoothness of a born gambler, he turned his attention to his mother-in-law and explained about his younger brother Nikos's wedding next week and how tonight's party was being held at Nikos's future in-laws' home, which was a half-hour's drive out of the city towards Corinth.

'You don't play fair,' Isobel told him in flat-toned Greek. 'You know I don't want to go.'

'What did you say?' her mother demanded.

'She said she didn't think it was fair to expect you to shop and spend the evening partying,' he lied smoothly. 'So we will solve the problem the rich man's way, and I will have a selection of evening gowns sent out here for you to peruse at your leisure.'

The *rich man* part was said to tease yet another smile from Silvia. The daughter didn't smile. But he did get a flashing vision of retribution to come. 'Try anything stupid just to get back at me, and I will retaliate,' he warned in Greek.

'What did *he* say?' Silvia wanted to know.

'He said choose something outrageously daring,' Isobel responded defiantly.

He laughed. What else could he do? He knew he had asked for that. It was fun having a wife that spoke his language, he decided.

But it was also time to cut and run, before she decided to corner him somewhere private and he did not get any work done today. Rising to his feet, he bid Silvia farewell and stepped round the table to kiss his wife's stiff cheek, then strode away, still feeling those wonderful barbs that had launched themselves at him.

'Don't you want to go to this party, Isobel?' her mother asked when she saw the way she glared at Leandros's retreating back.

Isobel turned her head to look at her mother, who had known about her problems with Leandros three years ago, but who had never been told about the problems Isobel had had with his family. 'I'm just a bit nervous about meeting people again,' she answered. 'It's too soon.'

'When you fall off a horse the best thing to do is get right back on it,' was her mother's blunt advice—while thoroughly ignoring the fact that mounting the dreaded horse had come about three years too late. 'And if I can see that you two looked so happy you have to be right for each other, then give other people the chance to make the same discovery,' she added sagely.

Isobel was about to open her mouth and tell her mother the hard facts about those other people, then changed her mind, because what was the use in stirring up trouble before it arrived? She was here—though she still wasn't sure how it had happened. She was staying—though she wished it didn't fill her with such a nagging ache of uncertainty.

Silvia sat back in her chair and released a happy sigh. 'Gosh, I feel reborn today,' she said. 'It makes me want to sing.'

She did sing—all morning. She loved every gown that

arrived—within the hour—complete with every accessory she could require. By the time Silvia went off for her afternoon siesta, Isobel was glad to escape to her room and wilt. But she couldn't wilt completely because she was expecting Leandros to walk in at any moment and she wanted to be ready for him.

However Leandros was running late. The few hours he had intended to spend at work had gone smoothly enough. Time began to get away from him when he went to the boot of his car to put away the briefcase he had left in his office the day before, and discovered that the jacket he had been wearing still lay where he had placed it before chasing after Isobel.He saw the edge of the envelope straight away. It was sticking out of one of the pockets but it was only when he reached down to slide it free that he remembered what it contained.

Two minutes later he was heading into the city, not out of it. A few minutes after that and he was striding into the bank with his wife's safety deposit box key and her letter authorising him to open the box. His curiosity was fully engaged as to what Isobel's idea of *family heirlooms* actually consisted of...

By the time he did eventually arrive home it was to find Isobel sitting cross-legged upon the bed, wearing what looked like one of his own white T-shirts—and nothing else from what he could see. She must have just come from the shower. Her hair was wet, and she was sitting with her head thrown forward while she combed the silken pelt with slow, smooth strokes, allowing the excess water to fall onto a white towel she had laid out in front of her.

'If you want a shower, I suggest you use a different bathroom,' she advised without lifting her head. 'Otherwise I might decide to murder you while you're naked and vulnerable in this one.'

He started to grin as he stood leaning in the doorway. In truth, after the trick he'd pulled this morning he had expected her to show her protest by refusing to come near this room.

'Not you, my sweet angel,' he denied lazily. 'You would see my quick death as being too kind to me.'

'Don't bank on it.'

'OK. I will live dangerously, then.' With that he levered away from the doorframe, came into the room and closed the door.

She still did not deign to lift her head as he walked across the room and placed two black velvet jewellery cases into the top drawer of a chest. Studying her as he removed his jacket and tie, he tried to decide whether to simply jump on her and give her no chance to defend herself, or whether to annoy her by ignoring her as she was ignoring him.

The former was tempting, but the latter should win since the shower seemed the best venue for the both of them. Her hair was wet already. The T-shirt belonged to him, and, having issued the threat, she would not, he knew, be able to remain sitting there passively without being drawn to carry out it out.

With a click and a scrape he undid his trousers and heeled off his shoes. Isobel's comb continued its smooth strokes while he removed his socks, then his under-shorts, which left only his shirt to conceal the fact that he was already very much aroused by this little game. He needed a shave so he strode into the danger-zone of the bathroom, paused long enough to reach in and spring the showerhead to life before he picked up his electric razor and began using it.

She arrived at the door as he had predicted, looked disconcerted to find him standing by the bathroom mirror, then mulish when she realised she had been outwitted by him.

'Choose your weapon,' he invited without allowing his eyes to leave the mirror, where his own reflection showed him a man who had changed a lot in the last twenty-four hours. Gone were the harsh lines of cynicism he had watched increase over the previous three years. Now he saw a pretty good-looking guy with a decent pair of shoulders and sexily provoking promise about him.

She did this for him, he acknowledged. This moody woman with the slicked-back wet hair and the sensationally smooth white skin.

She leapt without warning. Dropping the razor into the washbasin, he swung round in time to catch her against his chest. Green eyes glittered, her mouth quivered, her arms wrapped tightly around his neck.

'I don't want to go tonight!' she cried out plaintively.

She chose her weapon well. Anger he could deal with—a physical attack. But true tears and fear were different things entirely. 'Don't cry, *agape mou*. That isn't fair.'

'Can't we wait a few days before you toss me to the wolves again—please?' she begged.

The *please* almost unmanned him. He recovered while carrying her back to the bed. 'If anyone so much as glances at you wrongly I will strike them down, I promise you.'

'They can still think what they like about me, Andros!'

Andros; she was the only person to ever get away with calling him that, so when she did it, it turned his senses over, it tied possessive ropes around his heart. Vulnerable, cowardly, beautiful Isobel—the Isobel she let no one else ever see.

With grim intent he sat down on the bed then, as she still clung to him, he rolled them both backwards until they lay on their sides. 'Do you truly believe that we two are the only ones to regret what happened before?' he demanded. 'My mother had to watch me go to pieces. Within the year after you left I left here also and rarely ever came back again.'

'Where did you go?' She was diverted. He almost laughed at the irony. He revealed weakness and she suddenly became the strong one! 'To Spain,' he replied. 'To a place called San Estéban. I ran my companies from a stateroom on my yacht and learned to live with myself by pretending Athens didn't exist.'

'You should have come to me!' Her fist made contact with his shoulder. He trapped her beneath him on the bed. Her legs still clung though. She was not letting go of him and she was wearing nothing beneath the T-shirt.

'I did come to you,' he growled. 'Every night in my dreams!'

'Not good enough.'

'Then we have a lot of time to make up for,' he gritted and entered her—no preliminaries. Her cry was one of pleasure because she was ready to receive him. She clutched his head and brought his mouth crashing down onto hers. They rode the hot wind of raging passion. When it was over and he felt his strength return to him he got up as still she clung and walked them both beneath the shower, where he began the whole exhilarating ride all over again.

Getting ready to go out was not easy when he was feeling laid-back and slumberous. Fortunately, Isobel had wisely disappeared to the other bedroom so at least the temptation to forget tonight's party and remain lost in her was removed—in part. He was all too aware of that soft, pulsing sense of continued possession. He had only to think of her and he could imagine her crawling all over him in her desire to lay claim to every exquisitely receptive inch of his skin.

He grimaced as he retrieved the black jewellery cases from the chest of drawers, then went to find his red-haired tormentor. If she launched another attack on his defences, they would not be going anywhere, he promised his impatient senses.

CHAPTER EIGHT

HE ENTERED the room with a light tap to warn of his arrival. Isobel turned to the mirror to take one last look at herself and could not decide if she liked what she saw.

Nervous fingers fluttered down the short, close-fitting lined straight dress she had chosen to wear. It was made of a misty-jade silk-crêpe that clung sensually to her slender figure without being too obvious—she hoped. Her make-up was light and natural, her kitten-heeled lightweight mules matched the colour of the dress. But had she struck the note she had been striving for, in a different key to the old downright-provocative Isobel, without appearing as if she had conceded anything to the Greek idea of what was good taste?

'What do you think?' She begged his opinion while anxiety darkened her eyes and she wished to goodness that she'd worn her hair down—it had not occurred to her before that she liked to use her hair to hide behind and now she felt very exposed.

Leandros didn't reply, so she turned to gauge his expression, only to go breathlessly still when she found herself looking at a man from any warm-blooded woman's dreams. He'd discarded the conventional black dinner suit in favour of a white dinner jacket, black silk trousers and a black bow-tie. He looked smooth and dark and so sexually masculine that those tiny muscles inside her that were still gently pulsing from their last stimulation began to gather pace all over again.

His darkly hooded eyes moved over her in a way she

recognised only too well. Mine, the look said. 'Stunning,' he murmured. 'Nothing short of perfect.'

So are you, she was going to say, but as he walked towards her she noticed the black velvet jewellery cases in his hand and recognised them instantly.

Nervous fingers feathered the front of her dress again. 'S-so you got them back,' she said.

'The heirlooms?' His mouth twitched. 'As you see,' he confirmed easily.

With the neat flick of a finger he opened the flat case, gave her a few seconds to stare down at the platinum scrolls pierced with glowing emeralds and edged with sparkling diamonds that she had thought so beautiful when first she saw them. But that was before his sister's scornful, *'He's given you those old things? Mother always refused to wear them. Though they are definitely wasted on you,'* had taken their beauty away.

Now those same long fingers were lifting the necklace from its bed of velvet. 'Turn around,' he commanded.

'I…' Reluctance to so much as touch any of the pieces lying in that case was crawling across her skin. 'I gave you them back,' she pointed out edgily. 'I don't really want—'

'It has been a few eventful days filled with many second chances,' he replied in a light tone filled with sardonic dryness, 'for here I am, giving them back to you. They will be perfect with this lovely dress, don't you think?'

Maybe they would. 'But…' The necklace sparkled and glittered across the backs of his fingers. She lifted wary eyes to his and instantly felt as if she was drowning in a thick, dark sea of lazy indulgence. Let's go back to bed, she wanted to say. I feel safe there with you. 'Don't you think my wearing them tonight would be like slapping your family in the face with the fact that I am back? M-maybe I will wear them another time.'

'But you are back,' he pointed out with devastating simplicity. 'You are my beautiful wife. I gave these beautiful things to you and *I* want you to wear them. So turn around…'

She turned around, taking that sudden gleam of determination in his eyes with her. The necklace came to lie against her skin, circling the base of her throat as if it had been specially made to do so.

'A new beginning for you and I also mean a new beginning for everyone, *agape mou*,' he said deeply as she felt the warm press of his lips to her nape.

Then he was gently bringing her round to face him. With a neat flick the matching bracelet arrived around her slender wrist. Her stomach began to dance when he reached up to gently remove the tiny gold studs she was wearing in her ears. She could not believe there was another man alive who knew how to thread the fine hooks, from which there were suspended matching emerald-and-diamond-studded scrolls, into the piercing of a woman's ears without hurting.

He was standing so close—close enough for it to take only the slightest movement from her to close the gap. She stared at the sensual shape of his mouth and wanted badly to kiss it. Her breasts began to ache, her breathing shallowing out to hardly anything at all.

Flustered by her own crass lack of control around him, she turned away to stare into the mirror again. He was right about the jewellery looking perfect with the dress, she conceded reluctantly.

Her eyes flicked up to catch his in the mirror. He stood a head and the white-covered width of his shoulders taller than she did. She saw dark and light, frailty and strength.

They contrasted in every way there was, yet fitted together as if it had always meant to be this way.

'I still think that wearing these is like a slap in the face to your family,' she insisted.

Reaching up with a hand, he ran the gentle tip of a finger around the sparkling necklace. 'I think I am going to enjoy myself not too many hours from now.'

He was talking about sex on a bed draped with his wife wearing nothing but diamonds and emeralds. He was conjuring up enticing visions with which she didn't need any help to remember for herself. He laid a kiss upon her shoulder; she quivered, he sighed—then stepped away to pick up the other velvet box he had brought into the room with him.

She had forgotten all about it until he flicked up the lid. Her stomach was not the only thing to dance with fine flutters as he took a ring between finger and thumb. Ridding himself of the box, he slid the ring onto her finger until it came to rest against her wedding ring.

'This stays where it is,' he said very seriously.

The huge central stone seemed to issue a proclamation as he lifted it to his mouth. The diamonds framing the emerald almost blinded her beneath the overhead light. She might not know much about precious stones but she could recognise quality when she saw it.

'Who did these belong to—originally, I mean?' she asked curiously.

A mocking look appeared along with a lazy grin. 'The emeralds once belonged to a Venezuelan pirate who wore the one in the ring set into his front tooth.'

She laughed; it was irresistible not to at such an outrageous fairy tale. 'He would have had to have huge teeth!' she exclaimed.

'A swashbuckling, dark giant of a man with a black

velvet patch worn over one eye,' he embroidered shamelessly. Then, so unexpectedly it took her breath away, he bent to kiss her full on the mouth.

He stole her lipstick; she didn't care. He stole her every anxiety about tonight by reminding her of what really mattered. They left the bedroom hand in hand and walked down the stairs, meeting her mother, who was just making her way down the hallway, looking so lovely in her blue dress threaded with silver that her daughter stopped and sighed, 'Oh, Mum...'

The nerves returned when they turned into the driveway of a mansion house set in beautiful gardens lit to welcome its guests. Isobel's mother refused the use of her wheelchair, waving it away when their driver attempted to help her into it. Dignity and pride came before common sense tonight, though Silvia could not dismiss her need of her walking frame, no matter how independent she would prefer to be. However she was feeling buoyant and determined to enjoy herself.

Her daughter wished she could find the same motivation. Leandros's hand resting against her lower spine instilled some reassurance but the line-up of people waiting at the entrance was so daunting that Isobel was glad they were forced to take their time by matching their pace to her mother's slower steps.

She was introduced to Mr and Mrs Santorini and their daughter Carlotta, who was a lovely thing with dark hair and even darker liquid, smiling eyes. All three welcomed Isobel graciously but they were obviously curious about her, no matter how they tried to hide it. Nikos reminded her of Leandros when she had first met him, before life had got around to honing his handsome face. Nikos's smile was rueful as he greeted her with a lazy, 'Happy to see you here, Isobel.' As he bent to place a kiss on her cheek he added softly, 'And about time too.'

It was a nice thing for him to say, and helped to ease the next moment when Isobel had to face Leandros's mother. Thea looked stiff and awkward as she greeted the daughter-in-law who had been such a big disappointment to her. She was kind to Silvia, though, showed a genuine concern about her accident and promised to spend time with her later, catching up on what had happened.

'See, it wasn't so bad,' Leandros said quietly as they moved away.

'Only because you'd obviously primed them,' she countered.

The click of his tongue told her she had managed to annoy him. 'The chip on your shoulder must be very heavy, *agape*,' he drawled caustically, and the hand at her spine fell away. Feeling suddenly cast adrift as they stepped into a large reception room, Isobel then had to stand alone to deal with something like a hundred faces turning her way.

Some stared in open surprise, others glanced quickly down and away. Her skin began to prickle as the nerves she had been keeping under tight control broke free. Leandros could prime his family but he could not prime everyone, she noted painfully as the hiss of soft whispers suddenly attacked her burning ears.

It was awful. She felt that old familiar sensation as if she was beginning to shrink. With a lifting of her chin she stopped it from happening. Damn you all, her green eyes flashed.

Like the old times—like the old times, she chanted silently.

Her mother arrived at Leandros's other side, thankfully drawing some of the attention her way. Silvia, too, stopped to stare in surprise at what was taking place. 'Are we the star turn, Leandros?' she asked him. She wasn't a fool; her mother knew exactly what was going on here.

One of his hands went to cover one of Silvia's hands where it gripped the walking frame, the other arrived at Isobel's waist. Then he lifted his dark head to eye the room as a whole, and with a few economical movements he silenced whispers.

It came as a small shock to Isobel to see how much command he seemed to have over such an illustrious assembly. He had not warranted this much respect the last time she'd been here. Their three years apart had given him something extra she could only describe as presence. She had noticed it before in other ways but had not suspected that he could silence tongues with a single lift of his chiselled chin.

People went back to whatever they had been doing before they'd arrived to interrupt. Without uttering a word Leandros guided them towards a low sofa set against the nearest wall to them and quietly invited Silvia to sit. She shook her head. Like mother like daughter, Isobel mused ruefully. Neither of them was going to allow themselves to shrink here.

A waiter appeared to offer them tall flutes of champagne. Beginning to feel just a little bit nauseous, she allowed herself a tiny sip. 'OK?' Leandros murmured huskily.

'Yes,' she replied but they both knew she wasn't.

'I apologise for my earlier remark.' It was an acknowledgement that the chip-on-the-shoulder taunt had not been fair. 'I think I should have anticipated this. But, in truth, I did not expect them to be so...'

Rude, she finished for him. And—yes, he should have

expected it. But this was no time to jump into a row with him. That would come later, she promised herself.

'Isobel!' The call of her name brought her head up and the first genuine smile to widen her mouth. A diversion was coming in the shape of Eve Herakleides, who was bearing down upon them with her daunting giant of a grandfather and another man Isobel presumed must be Eve's new husband.

'Oh, this is just too good to be true!' Eve exclaimed as she arrived in front of them. Suddenly and intentionally, Isobel was sure, friendly, warm faces were surrounding them.

She and Eve shared kisses. Leandros was greeting Eve's grandfather—his uncle Theron—and introducing Theron to Silvia. Then Eve drew her husband forward and proudly presented him as her gorgeous Englishman. Ethan Hayes grimaced at being described in this way, but his eyes were smiling and his hand made its possessive declaration where it rested on Eve's slender waist.

Tensions began to ease as shifted they positions to complete introductions all round. Isobel found herself confronted by the great Theron Herakleides, who looked nothing like Leandros's mother. But then, they had been born several decades apart to different mothers. 'I am very happy to see you here,' he announced quite gravely, and bent to make the traditional two-kiss greeting.

Someone else arrived within their select little circle. It was Leandros's beautiful sister, Chloe, wearing an exquisite long and slinky gown of toreador red that set off her tall, dark, slender beauty to perfection. Her actions were stilted, the greeting she offered Isobel filled with the same awkward coolness as her mother's had been. Chloe was the youngest of the three Petronades children. All her life she had been adored and doted on by all the Petronades males, which in turn had made her spoiled and selfish, and she resented anyone who threatened to steal some of that adoration away from her.

She'd seen Isobel as one of those people. It still remained to be seen if Nikos's lovely Carlotta was going to be treated to the same petulant contempt. But, for now, Isobel was prepared to be polite and friendly—just in case Chloe had changed her attitude in the last three years.

Leandros saw his sister differently. Spoiled and selfish though she undoubtedly had been three years ago, she had gone through a very tough time after their father died. She'd worshipped him above all others, and losing him had left a huge gap in her heart that she'd looked to him and Nikos to fill. When he'd married Isobel, Chloe had taken this as yet another devastating loss and had fiercely resented Isobel for being the cause.

Chloe had changed over the last three years though. Grown up, he supposed, and was less of a spoiled little cat. Though he understood that Isobel didn't know that—which was why he felt her fingers searching for the secure comfort of his hand as Chloe levelled her dark eyes upon her and said, 'Welcome home, Isobel,' then concluded the greeting with a kiss to both of Isobel's cheeks with a very petulant mouth.

He was about to offer a wry smile at this bit of petulance, when something else happened to wipe out all hint of humour. As she drew away Chloe's gaze flickered down to the jewels flashing at Isobel's throat and a faint flush was suddenly staining her elegant cheekbones as she looked away in clear discomfort.

He had his culprit, he realised grimly.

The ever-sharp Eve also noticed Chloe's fleeting glance at Isobel's throat—and her ensuing discomfort. The little minx made a play of checking out Isobel's necklace. 'Oh, how lovely,' she declared. 'Are they old or are they new?'

'Most definitely new,' Leandros answered smoothly. 'I had them specially commissioned for Isobel just after we were married,' he explained. 'As far as I recall Isobel has only worn them once before—isn't that so, *agape mou*?'

'I... Yes.' He watched her fingers jerk up to touch the necklace. She was trying to hide her shock at what he had said, while his sister had turned to a block of stone.

'We like to call them the family heirlooms.' Oh, cruelty be mine, he thought with grim satisfaction as he soothed Isobel with the gentle squeeze of her hand and smiled glassily into his sister's unblinking eyes. Chloe realized that he now knew the kind of unkind rubbish she had fed to his wife. She also now realized that she was in deep trouble the next time he got her alone. He was looking forward to it, Chloe certainly wasn't.

The buffet dinner was announced. Maybe it was fortunate because it gave his darling sister the excuse to melt away. People shifted positions as the slow mass exodus to the adjoining room began. Eve strolled away with her husband. Theron was gallantly offering to escort Isobel's mother. They went off together, Theron matching his long strides to Silvia's smaller steps while talking away to her with an easy charm.

Which left them alone again. 'I think Theron has taken to your mother,' he observed lightly.

'Just don't speak,' his wife told him stiffly. 'I'm too angry to listen to you.'

He looked down into glinting eyes. 'Why, what have I done?' he asked innocently.

'You don't have to do anything to be a horrible person,' she answered. 'It must be in the genes.'

'Then you understand why my sister is the way that she

is,' he countered smoothly, and when she went to stalk away from him he stopped her by tightening his grip on her hand. 'We do not run away any more, *agape mou*,' he reminded her.

'Sometimes I can hate you.' Her chin was up. 'All the time you were dressing me up in these, you were laughing at me!'

He laughed now, low and huskily. She was beginning to sizzle. He loved it when she sizzled. 'The Venezuelan pirate was pure inspiration.' Another flash sparked from her eyes and he should have been slain where he stood. 'Now tell me the fairy tale Chloe fed to you.'

Her mouth snapped shut in refusal to answer. 'Loyalty from the witch for the cat?' he drawled quizzically. 'Now, that does surprise me.'

Isobel had surprised herself. She had a suspicion her silence had something to do with the pained look she'd seen on Chloe's face as Leandros taunted her, and the fact that Chloe had flicked her a glance of mute apology before she'd slipped away.

'I'm hungry,' she said, which could not be less true since she knew she would not be able to swallow a single thing tonight. But the claim served its purpose in letting him know that a discussion about his sister was not going to happen. Not until she understood where Chloe was coming from these days. It was Leandros who wanted her to give his family a chance, after all.

'Why Venezuelan?' she asked suddenly. 'Why not French or Spanish or—?'

His laughter sent his dark head back. People turned to stare as if they weren't used to hearing him laugh like this. He deigned not to notice their disconcerted glances, kissed her full on her mouth then led her to join the crush around the buffet table.

The evening moved on. With a quiet determination, Leandros took her from group to group and pulled her into conversation in a way that she could only describe as making a statement about the solidarity of their marriage. As he did this he also exposed yet another secret, by always making sure he made some remark to her in Greek. By the time a couple of hours had gone by there wasn't a person present who had known her before who did not know now that she understood their native tongue.

And he had done it with such ruthless intention. Leandros was making sure that people thought twice before discussing his wife in her presence. Some looked uncomfortable at the discovery; some simply accepted it with pleased surprise. The uncomfortable ones were logged in his memory; Isobel could almost see him compiling a list of those people who would not be included in their social circle in the future.

Other people made sure they kept their distance, which spoke even greater volumes about what they were thinking. Takis Konstantindou was one of those people. Chloe, of course, was another one. She could understand Chloe's reasons for steering clear of them but the lawyer's cool attitude puzzled her.

Then there was Diantha Christophoros. If Isobel glimpsed her at all it was usually within a group that contained either Chloe or Leandros's mother. In a way she could find it in herself to feel sorry for Diantha, because it couldn't have been easy for her to turn up here tonight knowing that everyone here was going to know by now that old rumours about Leandros wanting to divorce his wife to marry her had to be false.

'Don't you think we should go and speak to her?' she suggested when she caught Leandros glancing Diantha's way.

'For what purpose?' he questioned coolly.

'She has got to be feeling uncomfortable, Leandros. The rumours affect her as much as they do you.'

'The best way to kill a rumour is to starve it,' was his response. 'Diantha seems to have my sister and my mother to offer all the necessary comfort.'

Which said, more or less, what Isobel had been trying *not* to think. The family preference could not be more noticeable if they stuck signs on their backs saying 'Vote Isobel out and Diantha in'. It was Eve Herakleides who put it in an absolute nutshell when she came to join Isobel out on the terrace, where she'd slipped away to get some fresh air that did not contain curiosity and intrigue.

'Word of warning,' Eve began. 'Watch out for Diantha Christophoros. She may appear nice and quiet and amiable but she has hidden talents behind the bland smile. She has a way of manipulating people without them realising she's doing it. It was only a few weeks ago that she convinced Chloe that she should remain here to help her mother with Nikos's wedding arrangements, while Diantha went to Spain in Chloe's place to help Leandros with a big celebration party he threw in San Estéban. Chloe puzzled for ages afterwards as to how it had actually come about that she'd agreed, since she had been so looking forward to spending two weeks with her brother. Then, blow me if Diantha isn't back in Athens for less than a day when the rumours were suddenly flying about Leandros filing for divorce from you so that he could marry her. She wants your husband,' she announced sagely. 'And her uncle Takis wants her to have him.'

'Takis and Diantha are related?' It was news to Isobel.

Eve nodded. 'They're a tightly knit lot, these upper-crust Greeks,' she said candidly. 'Thank goodness for women like you and my mother or they'd be so inbred they would have wiped themselves out by now.'

'What a shocking thing to say!' Isobel gasped on a compulsive giggle.

'And what shocking thing is this minx saying now?' Leandros intruded.

A pair of hands arrived at Isobel's slender waistline, the brush of his lips warmed her cheek—the lick of his tongue against her earlobe as he pulled away again sent her wretched knees weak.

'Woman-talk is for women only,' the minx answered for herself. 'And you, dear cousin, have had a lucky escape in my opinion.' With that provocatively cryptic remark, she walked away.

They both turned to watch her go, an exquisite creature dressed in slinky hot pink making a direct line for her husband, who sensed her coming—his broad shoulders gave a small shake just before he turned around and grinned.

'She hooked him in against his will,' Leandros confided. 'I think he still finds it difficult to believe that he let her do it.'

'Well, I think he's a very lucky man,' Isobel stated loyally because she liked Eve and always had done.

'Mmm,' he murmured, 'so am I...'

'No—don't,' she breathed when he began to lower his dark head again. 'Not here; you will ruin what bit of dignity I have managed to maintain.'

His warm laughter teased as he used his grip on her waist to swing her round until her hips rested against the heavy stone balustrade behind her. His superior bulk was suddenly hiding her from view of everyone else. Eyes like molasses began sending the kind of messages that forced her to lower her gaze from him.

'I like you in this,' she murmured softly, running her fingers beneath the slender lapels of his white jacket.

'Tell me I look like a Greek waiter and I will probably toss you over this balustrade,' he warned.

Her smile appeared wrapped in rueful memories of the time she had once said that to him in an attempt to flatten his impossible ego. 'I was such a bitch,' she confessed.

'No,' Leandros denied that. 'You assured me at the time that you had a hot thing for Greek waiters. I think I was supposed to feel complimented,' he mused thoughtfully.

It was irresistible; she just had to lift her laughing eyes upwards again. It was a mistake. She just fell into those eyes filled with such warm, dark promises. Her breath began to feather, a new kind of tension began circling them like a sensual predator circling its two victims while inside the house, beyond the pair of open terrace doors, a party was taking place. Music was filtering out to them on the warm summer air along with laughter and the general hum of conversation.

'I love you,' she said. It came out of nowhere.

He responded with a sharp intake of breath. His shoulders tensed, his whole body stiffened, his grip tightened on her waist. 'Fine time to tell me that!' he snapped out thinly. But he wasn't angry, just—overwhelmed.

She began to tremble because it had been such a dangerous thing for her to say out loud. It committed her, totally and utterly. It stood her naked and exposed and so vulnerable to hurt again that her throat locked up on a bank of emotion which threatened to turn into tears.

He was faring no better. She could feel the struggle he was having with himself not to respond in some wildly passionate way. A verbal response would have been enough for Isobel. A simple, 'I love you too,' would have helped her through this.

'I'll take it back if you like,' she shot out a trifle wildly.

'No,' he rasped. 'Just don't speak again while I…'

Deal with this; she finished the sentence for him. It was silly; it was stupid. They were grown-ups who were supposed to have a bit more class than to put each other through torture in public. She couldn't stop herself from flicking a glance at his face. As she did so he looked down. A wave of feeling washed over both of them in a static-packed blowback from just three little words.

They could have been alone. They *should* have been alone. Her breasts heaved on a tense pull of air. His hands pulled her hard against him. 'Don't kiss me!' she shot out in a constrained choke.

'The balustrade is still very tempting,' he gritted. 'I thought Eve was the biggest minx around here but you knock her into a loop.'

Heat was coursing through her body; the shocking evidence that he was on fire for her was shutting down her brain. The music played, the laughter and hum of conversation swirled all around them. In a minute, she had a horrible suspicion, she was going to find herself flattened to the ground with this big, lean, suave and sophisticated man very much on top.

'All sweetness and light,' he continued, thrusting the words down at her from between clenched teeth. 'All smiles and quiet answers for everyone else. The hair is up, so neat and prim—since when did you ever give way to such convention? Everyone back there sees the beautifully refined version of Isobel but I have to get the tormenting witch!'

'Keep talking,' she encouraged. She was beginning to get angry now. 'If you do it for long enough maybe you will wear yourself out!'

'I am not wearing out.' He took her words literally. 'I

am just getting started. From the moment you strode back into my life on those two sensational legs of yours you've had me standing on pins like some love-lost fool with no idea what is happening to me.'

'Did you dare use the love word then?' she taunted glacially.

'I've *always* loved you!' he thrust out harshly. 'I loved you when we flirted across the top of a Ferrari. I still loved you when you left me pining for three damn years!'

'Three years of pining,' she mocked unsteadily. 'I didn't see any evidence of it.' But he'd said it. He had actually said it.

'We've been through that already,' he snapped out impatiently.

'You brought me back here to divorce me.'

'It was an excuse. Anyone with sense would have realised that.'

'You had your next wife all picked out and ready.'

'I am arrogant. You know I am arrogant. Can you not cut a man a bit of slack?'

'Which is why I had to say it first, I suppose.'

The air hissed from between his teeth. If an electric cable had been fitted to them, they could have lit up the night there was so much static stress.

'I think the *both* of us are about to go over this balustrade,' he gritted furiously.

'You will go first,' Isobel vowed. 'And I hope you break your arrogant neck!'

A sound behind them brought them swinging round in unison. Isobel's heart sank to her shoes when she saw her mother-in-law hovering a few yards away. What did they look like? What did she see? Two people locked in a row that probably brought back a hundred memories of similar rows like this? She looked wary and anxious, her black eyes flicking from one to the other. Oh, God, please help me, Isobel groaned silently.

'I am sorry to intrude,' Thea said stiffly, and her gaze finally settled upon Isobel's blushing face. 'But I am concerned about your mama, Isobel. Theron has her dancing with her walking frame and I am afraid his enthusiasm is tiring her out.'

A single glance through the doors into the house was all that was needed to confirm that Thea's concerns were real. The seventy-year-old Theron was indeed dancing with her mother, who was using the walking frame as a prop. The man was flirting outrageously. Silvia was laughing, enjoying herself hugely, but even from here Isobel could see the strain beginning to show on her face.

'I'll go and…' She went to move, but Leandros stopped her.

'No, let me. She will take the disappointment better if I do it,' he insisted. At Isobel's questioning glance, 'Two men fighting over her?' he explained quizzically, then dropped a kiss on her lips and strode off, pausing only long enough to drop a similar kiss on his mother's cheek.

Suddenly Isobel found herself alone with a woman who did not like her. Awkwardness became a tangible thing that held them both silent and tense.

'My son is very fond of your mother.' Thea broke the silence with that quiet observation.

'Yes.' Isobel's eyes warmed as she watched Leandros fall into a playful fight with Theron for Silvia's hand. 'My mother is fond of him, too.'

She hadn't meant it as a strike at their cold relationship but she realised that Thea had taken it that way as she stiffened and turned to leave. 'No, don't go, please,' she murmured impulsively.

Her mother-in-law paused. An ache took up residence

inside Isobel's chest. This was supposed to be a time for fresh starts and for Leandros's sake she knew she had to try to reach out with the hand of friendship.

'You were arguing again.' Once again it was Thea who took up the challenge by spinning to face her with the accusation.

'You misread what you saw,' Isobel replied, then offered up a rueful smile. 'We were actually making love.' Adding a shrug to the smile, she forced herself to go on. 'It has always been like this between us. We spark each other off. Sometimes I think we could light the whole world up with the power we can generate...' Her eyes glazed on a wistful float back to what Thea had interrupted. Then she blinked into focus. 'Though I understand why you might not have seen it like that,' she was willing to concede.

Her mother-in-law took a few moments to absorb all of this, then she sighed and some of the tension dropped out of her stiff shoulders. 'I understand that you learned Greek while you were here the last time.'

'Yes,' Isobel confirmed.

'I think, perhaps, that you therefore heard things said that should not have been said.'

Lowering her gaze. 'Yes,' she said again.

Another small silence followed. Then Thea came to stand by the balustrade. 'My son loves you,' she said quietly. 'And Leandros's happiness is all I really care about. But the fights...' She waved a delicately structured hand in a gesture of weariness. 'They used to tire me out.'

And me, Isobel thought, remembering back to when the sparks were not always so lovingly passionate.

'When you left here, I was relieved to see you go. But Leandros did not feel the same. He was so miserable here that he went to Spain on a business trip and did not come back again. He missed you.'

'I missed him too.'

'Yes…' Thea accepted that. 'Leandros wants us to be friends,' she went on. 'I would like that too, Isobel.'

Though Thea's tone warned that she was going to have to work at it. Isobel smiled; what else could she do? Her mother-in-law was a proud woman. She was making a climb-down here that took with it some of that pride.

Taking in a deep breath, she gave that pride back to her. 'I was too young four years ago. I was overwhelmed by your lifestyle, and too touchy and too rebellious by far to accept advice on how best to behave or cope.' Lifting her eyes to Leandros's mother's eyes, 'This time will be different,' she promised solemnly.

Her mother-in-law nodded and said nothing. They both knew they had reached some kind of wary compromise. As she turned to go back to the party Thea paused. 'I am sorry about the baby,' she said gravely. 'It was another part of your unhappiness here, because kindness was not used to help you through the grief of your loss.'

It was so very true that there really was no ideal answer to give to that. Her mother-in-law seemed to realise it, and after another hesitation she walked back into the house.

Leandros appeared seconds later and Isobel had to wonder if he had been leaving them alone to talk. He searched her face. 'OK?' he asked huskily.

She nodded, then had to step up to him and, sliding her arms inside his jacket and around his back, she pressed herself against his solid strength. 'Don't ever let me go again,' she told him.

'I won't.' It was a promise.

They left the party soon after that, making the journey home without speaking much. The talking was left to

Silvia, who chattered away about Theron and the plans he had to take her out tomorrow for the day.

'I can't believe it,' Isobel said to Leandros as they prepared for bed. 'My mother has caught the eye of the wealthiest man in Greece!'

'His roving eye,' Leandros extended lazily. 'My uncle Theron is an established rake.'

'But he's got to be seventy years old! Surely he can't be looking at my mother and seeing...'

Her voice trailed away in dismay as a dark eyebrow arched. 'I share the same blood.' He began to stalk her with a certain gleam in his eyes. She was wearing nothing but the family heirlooms. 'Do you think you will be able to keep up with me when I reach seventy and you will be...?'

'Don't you dare tell me how old I will be!' she protested.

But, as for the rest, well, she was more than able to keep up with him throughout the long, dark, silken night. This time it was different, like a renewal of vows they made to each other four distant years ago. There were no secrets left to hide, just love and trust and a desire to hold on to what they had found.

The morning brought more sunshine with it and breakfast laid out on the terrace for two. Silvia was taking breakfast in her room today before she got ready for her date. When it came time for Leandros to go and spend a few essential hours in his office, he left her with a reluctance that made her smile. Theron arrived. A big, silver-thatched, larger-than-life kind of man, he was polite to Isobel, flirtatious with her mother and somehow managed to convince Silvia that her wheelchair was required today, which earned him a grateful smile from Silvia's daughter.

Left to her own devices, Isobel asked Allise for a second

pot of tea, then sat back in her chair and tried to decide what she wanted to do with the few hours she had going spare while Leandros wasn't here.

She was wearing the green combat trousers and a yellow T-shirt today. The sum total of the wardrobe she had brought with her from England had now been exhausted and she was considering going out to do a bit of shopping, when Allise arrived with the promised pot of tea and an envelope that she said had just been delivered by hand.

Maybe Isobel should have known before she even touched it that it could only mean trouble. Everything was just too wonderful, much too perfect to stay that way. But the envelope did not come with WARNING printed on it, just her name typed in its centre and the fizz of intrigue because she could think of only one person who would do this, and he had been gone only half an hour.

He was up to something—a surprise, she decided, and was smiling as she split the seal.

But what fell into her hands had her smile dying. What she found herself looking at had her fingers tossing the photographs away from her as if she were holding a poisonous snake and she lurched to her feet with enough violence to send crockery spilling to the ground. Her chair toppled over with a clatter against the hard tile flooring, her hand shot up to cover her shaking mouth. Her heart was pounding, eyes that had been shining were now dark with a horror that was curdling the blood.

She stepped back, banged her leg on the upturned chair. She was going to be sick, she realised—and ran.

CHAPTER NINE

ALLISE found Isobel sitting on the floor of the bathroom which lay just off the terrace, her cheek resting against the white porcelain toilet bowl. On a cry of dismay the house-keeper hurried forward. '*Kyria,* you are ill!'

It was a gross understatement. Isobel was dying inside and she didn't think she was going to be able to stop it from happening.

'I get the doctor—the *kyrios.*'

'No!' Isobel exploded on a thrust of frail energy. 'No.' She tried to calm her voice when Allise stood back and stared at her. 'I'm all right,' she insisted. 'I just need to— lie down for a wh-while.'

Dragging herself to her feet, she had to steady herself at the washbasin before she could get her trembling legs to work. Stumbling out of the bathroom, she headed for the stairs, knew she would never make it up there and changed direction, making dizzily for the only sanctuary her instincts would offer up as an alternative—her mother's room.

Back to the womb, she likened it starkly as she felt the housekeeper's worried eyes watch her go. She was going to ring him; Isobel was sure of it. Allise would feel she had failed in her duty if she did not inform Leandros as to what she had seen.

But Leandros didn't need informing. At about the time that Isobel received her envelope, he was receiving one himself. As he stared down at the all-too-damning photo-graphs the phone began to ring. It was Diantha's father;

161

he had received an envelope too. Hot on that call came one from his mother, then an Athens newspaper with a hungry reputation for juicy gossip about the jet set. It did not take a genius to know what was unfolding here.

Leandros was on his way home even as Isobel paused at the table where the photographs lay amongst the scattered crockery. His mobile phone was ringing its cover off. With an act of bloody, blinding frustration he switched it off and tossed it onto the passenger seat with the envelope of photos. Whoever else had received copies could go to hell because if he was certain about anything, then it was that Isobel had to be looking at the same ugly evidence.

His car screeched to a halt in the driveway, kicking up clouds of dust in its wake. He left the engine running as he strode into the house. Watching him go, the gardener went to switch off the engine for him, his eyes filled with frowning puzzlement. Allise was standing in the hall with her ear to the telephone.

'Where is my wife?' he demanded and was already making for the stairs when the housekeeper stopped him.

'Sh-she is in her mama's rooms, *kyrios*.'

Changing direction, he headed down the hallway. He lost his jacket as he hit the terrace. His tie went and he was about to stride past the debacle that was the breakfast table and chairs, when he saw the envelope and scatter of photographs, felt sickness erupt in his stomach and anger follow it with a thunderous roar.

Pausing only long enough to gather up the evidence, he continued down the terrace and into the rooms allotted to his mother-in-law. He had not been in here since Silvia took up residence and was surprised how comfortable she had managed to make it, despite the clutter of Isobel's photographic equipment still dotted around. Not that he cared about comfort right now, for across the room, lying curled on her mother's bed like a foetus, was his target.

His heart tipped sideways on a moment of agony—then it grimly righted again. Snapping the top button of his shirt free with angry fingers, he approached the bed with a look upon his face that promised retribution for someone very soon.

'Isobel.' He called her name.

She gave no indication that she had even heard him. Was she waiting for him to go down on his knees to beg for understanding and forgiveness? Well, not this man, he thought angrily and tossed the photographs down beside her on the bed.

'These are false,' he announced. 'And I expect you to believe it.'

It was a hard, tough, outright challenge. Still she did not even offer a deriding sob in response. It made him want to jump inside her skin so that she would *know* he could not have done this terrible thing.

'Isobel!' he rasped. 'This is no time for dramatics. You are the trained photographer. I need you to tell me how they did it so I can strangle the culprit with their lies.'

'Go away,' she mumbled.

On a snap of impatience, he bent and caught hold of her by her waist, then lifted her bodily off the bed before firmly resettling her sitting on its edge. Going down on his haunches, he pushed the tumble of silken hair back from her face. She was as white as a sheet and her eyes looked as if someone had reached in and hollowed them out.

'Now just listen,' he insisted.

Her response was to launch an attack on him. He supposed she had the right, he acknowledged as he grimly held on to her until she had finally worn herself out. Eventually she sobbed out some terrible insult then tried scrambling backwards in an effort to get away. Her fingers made contact with the photographs. On a sob she picked them up.

'You lied to me!' she choked out thickly. 'You said she meant nothing to you but—look—*look*!' The photographs shook as she brandished them in his grim face. 'You, standing on your yacht w-wearing nothing from what I can see, h-holding her in front of you while she's just about covered by th-that excuse for a slip!'

'It never—'

The photograph went lashing by his cheek, causing him to take avoiding action, and by the time he had recovered she was staring at the next one. 'Look at you,' she breathed in thick condemnation. 'How can you lie there with her, sleeping like an innocent? I will never forgive you—'

She was about to send the images the way of the other when he snaked out a hand and took the rest from her. 'You will believe me when I say these are not real!' he insisted harshly.

Not real? Isobel stared at him through tear-glossed eyes and wondered how he dared say that when each picture was now branded on her brain!

'I believed you when you said you hadn't—'

'Then continue to believe,' he cut in. 'And start thinking with your head instead of your heart.'

'I don't have a heart,' she responded. 'You ripped it out of my body and threw it away!'

'Melodrama is not helping here, *agape*,' he sighed, but she saw the hint of humour he was trying to keep from showing on his lips.

That humour was her complete undoing, and she began wriggling and squirming until he finally set her free to stand.

'I'm leaving here,' she told him as she swung to her feet.

'Running again?' he countered jeeringly. 'Take care,' he warned as he rose up also, 'because I might just let you do it. For I will *not* live my life fearing the next time you are going to take to your feet and flee!'

Isobel stared at him, saw the sheer black fury darkening his face. 'What are you angry with me for?' she demanded bewilderedly.

'I am not angry with you,' he denied. 'I am angry with—these.' He waved a hand at the photographs. 'You are not the only one to receive copies...' Then he told her who else had. 'This is serious, Isobel,' he imparted grimly. 'Someone is out to cause one hell of a scandal and I need your help here, not your contempt.'

With that he turned and began looking around the room with hard, impatient eyes. Spotting whatever it was he was searching for, he strode over to her old computer system and began checking that everything was plugged in. 'You know how to do this better than I do,' he said. 'Show me what I need to do to bring this thing to life.'

'It hasn't been used for three years. It has probably died from lack of use.'

'At least try!' he rasped.

It was beginning to get through to her that he was deadly serious. Moving on trembling legs and with an attitude that told him she was not prepared to drop her guard, she went to stand beside him. With a flick of a couple of switches she then stood back to wait. It was quite a surprise to watch a whole array of neglected equipment burst into life.

'Now what?' she asked stiffly.

'Scan those photographs into the relevant program,' he instructed. 'Blow them up—or whatever it is you do to them so we can study them in detail.'

'A reason would be helpful.'

'I have already told you once. They are fakes.'

'Sure?'

He swung on her furiously. 'Yes, I am sure! And I would appreciate a bit of trust around here!'

'If you shout at me once more I will walk,' she threatened fiercely.

'Then stop looking at me as if I am a snake; start using a bit of sense and believe me!' Striding off, he recovered the photographs—yet again. Coming back, he set them down next to the computer screen.

'Fakes, you say,' she murmured.

'Do your magic and prove me right or wrong.'

The outright challenge. Still without giving him the benefit of the doubt, she opened the lid on the flatbed scanner and prepared to work. Her mouth was tight, her eyes were cold, but with a few deft clicks of the mouse she began to carry out his instructions. If he was lying then he had to know she would find him out in a few minutes. If he was telling the truth then...

Her stomach began to churn. She was no longer sure which alternative she preferred. It was one thing believing that your estranged husband had been involved in an affair during your separation but it was something else entirely to know that someone was willing to go to such extremes to hurt other people.

'Why is this happening?' she questioned huskily. 'Who do you think it is that took these? It needs a third party involved to take photographs like these, Leandros. Someone close enough to you to be in a position to catch you on film like this.'

He was standing to one side of her and she felt him stiffen; glancing up, she caught a glimpse of his bleak expression before he turned away. 'Chloe, of course,' he answered gruffly.

Chloe? 'Oh, no.' She didn't want to believe that. Not Chloe, who adored her brother. 'She has nothing to gain by hurting both you and her best friend!'

'She gains what she's always wanted,' he countered tightly. 'Work—work!' he commanded as the first photograph appeared on the screen. Turning back, she clicked the mouse and the picture leapt to four times its original size. 'All her childhood she fantasised about one of her brothers marrying her best friend,' he continued darkly. 'Nikos and I have ruined those fantasies, so now she is out for revenge.'

'I don't want to believe it.'

'She has also been cleverer than I ever gave her credit for,' he added cynically. 'She damns me in your eyes. Damns both Diantha and me to Diantha's father, who honoured me with his trust when he allowed her to stay on my yacht with me. I saw a man taking photographs of the yacht from the quay. This one,' he flicked a finger at the screen, 'Shows exactly how I was dressed that day.'

'In nothing?'

'I have a pair of shorts on, you sarcastic witch!' He scowled. 'He had to have been paid by someone. Scheming Chloe is the logical person. Her ultimate aim is to see you walking off with a divorce and me being forced into marrying Diantha to save her reputation!'

'All of that is utterly nonsensical!' Isobel protested. 'No one goes to such drastic extremes on someone else's behalf.'

'Who else's behalf?' he challenged. 'Diantha's? She is being manipulated here just as ruthlessly as we are,' he insisted. 'Look at the evidence. Chloe sends Diantha in her stead to San Estéban. These photographs were taken there. I actually saw the guy taking this one!'

'And the one in your bedroom?' she prompted. 'How did he get in there?'

He paused to frown at the question. Then the frown cleared. 'He has to be a member of my crew,' he decided. 'He was too far away for me to recognise him.'

He thought he had an answer for everything. But Isobel was recalling a conversation with Eve Herakleides the night before, and suddenly she had a very different suspect to challenge Leandros's claims.

Flattening her lips and concentrating her attention on the screen, she took only seconds to spot the first discrepancy. Within a few minutes she had circled many—a finger missing, a point on the yacht's rail that did not quite fit. With the mouse flying busily, she copied then pasted each detail onto a separate frame, increased their size then sent them to print.

Through it all Leandros watched in silent fascination as the whole photograph was broken down and revealed for the fraud that it was. 'Do you want me to do the same to the rest of them?' she asked when she'd finished.

'Not unless you need to assure yourself that they are all fakes,' he responded coolly, gathering up his precious evidence.

It was a clean hit on her lack of trust. Isobel acknowledged it with a sigh. 'I suppose you want me to eat humble pie now.'

'Later,' he replied. 'Humble pie will not come cheap.'

But neither smiled as he said it. Fakes or not, the photographs had stolen something from them and Isobel had to ask herself if they were ever going to get it back again.

'Leandros…' He was striding for the door when she

stopped him. 'Chloe knows what I do for a living; remember that when you confront her.'

'Meaning what?' He glanced at her.

Isobel shrugged. 'Just go there with an open mind, that's all,' she advised. It wasn't up to her to shatter his faultless image of Diantha. And, anyway, she wasn't sure enough of her own suspicions to make an issue out of it.

But she was as determined as he was to find out.

He had been gone for less than two minutes before she was printing off her second lot of copies. His car was only just turning off the driveway when she was calling a taxi for herself. The Christophoros mansion was much the same as most of the houses up here on the hill. She was greeted by a maid who showed her into a small reception room, then hurried off to get the daughter of the house.

Diantha took her time. Needing something to do, Isobel reached into her bag to search out a hair-band and snapped her hair into a pony-tail. Leandros would see this as her donning her tough-lady persona, but she didn't feel tough. Her nerves were beginning to fray, her stomach dipping and diving on lingering nausea. She didn't know if she had done the right thing by coming here, wasn't even sure how she was going to tackle this—all she did know with any certainty was that Diantha had to be faced, whether guilty or innocent.

The door began to open and she swung round as Diantha appeared looking neat in a mid-blue dress and wearing a thoroughly bland expression that somehow did not suit the occasion, bearing in mind that Isobel could be a jealous wife come here to tear her limb from limb.

Indeed Diantha looked her over as if she were the marriage breaker in this room. 'We will have to make this brief.' There was a distinct chill to her tone. 'My father is on his way home and he will not like to find you here.'

Then she really took the wind out of Isobel's sails when she added smoothly, 'Now you have seen the truth about Leandros and myself, can we hope that you will get out of our lives for good?'

Isobel's fingers tightened on the shoulder strap to her bag. 'So it was you who sent the photographs?' she breathed.

Diantha's cool nod confirmed it. It seemed a bit of a let-down that she was admitting it so easily. 'Though I must add that anything I say to you here I will deny to anyone else,' she made clear. 'But you are in the way, and I am sick of being messed around by Leandros. Two weeks ago he was promising me he would divorce you and marry me, then I am being sidelined—for business reasons, of course; isn't it always?'

'Business reasons?' Isobel prompted curiously.

'The lack of a pre-nuptial agreement between the two of you put Leandros in an impossible situation.'

It was like being in the presence of some deadly force, Isobel thought with a shiver. Diantha was calm, her voice was level and Isobel could already feel herself being manipulated by the gentle insertion of the word pre-nuptial. Before she knew it Lester Miles' warnings about the power of her own position came back to haunt her. She was seeing Leandros's sudden change from a man ready to sever a marriage to a man eager to hang on to that marriage.

'I have to say that I am seriously displeased at being forced to lie about our relationship while he sorts out this mess,' Diantha continued. 'But a man with his wealth cannot allow himself to be ripped off by a greedy wife. Nor can he afford to risk our two family names being thrown into the public arena with a scandal you will cause if you wish to turn your divorce ugly. But you mark my words, Kyria Petronades, a contract will appear before very soon, mapping out the details of any settlements in the event of your marriage reaching a second impasse.'

'But you couldn't wait that long,' Isobel inserted. 'So you decided to cause the feared scandal and get it out of the way?'

'I am sick of having to lie to everyone,' she announced. 'It is time that people knew the truth.'

'About your affair in Spain with my husband,' Isobel prompted.

'A relationship that began long before you left him, if you must know the truth.' Her chin came up. 'He visited me in Washington, DC.'

Isobel remembered the Washington trips all too well.

'Our two weeks spent in Spain were not the first stolen weeks we managed to share together. I have no wish to hurt your feelings with this, but he was with me only yesterday, during siesta. We have an apartment in Athens where we meet most days of the week.'

'No photographic evidence of these meetings?' Isobel challenged.

'It can be arranged.'

'Oh, I am sure that it can.' And she removed the print-outs from her handbag and placed them down on the table that stood between them. Believing she knew exactly what she was being presented with, Diantha didn't even deign to look.

'You are nothing but a lying, conniving bitch, Diantha,' Isobel informed her. 'You manipulate people and *adore* doing it. Chloe was manipulated to get you to Spain. My mother-in-law has been beautifully manipulated by your ever-so-gentle eagerness to please and offer her up an easier alternative to me as the daughter-in-law from hell.'

'You said it,' Diantha responded, revealing the first hint that a steel-trap mind functioned behind the bland front.

Isobel laughed. 'Leandros extols you for your great organisational skills—not a very appetising compliment to the woman he loves, is it?' she added when Diantha's spine made a revealing shift. 'Apparently you know how to put together a great party.' She dug her claws in. 'As for me, well, I struggle to organise anything, but he calls me a witch and a hellion and claims I have barbs for teeth. When we make love he falls apart in my arms and afterwards he sleeps wrapped around me. Not like this.' She stabbed a finger at the photograph. 'Not with him occupying one side of the bed while I occupy the other.'

Black eyelashes flickered downwards, her face kept firmly under control. Now she had drawn her attention to the photographs, Isobel slid out the other one, and its enlarged partners in crime. 'Thankfully, Leandros still has *all* his fingers.' She stabbed one of her own fingers on the missing one splayed across Diantha's stomach. 'If he stood behind you like this, the top of your head would reach no higher than his chest, not his chin. You are short in stature, Diantha—let's call a spade a spade here, since you wish to talk bluntly. You are not quite this slim or this curvaceous. And when you cut, shave and paste with a computer mouse it is always advisable to make sure you fill in the gaps you make, like the yacht rail here, which seems to stop for no apparent reason. A good manipulator should always be sure of all her facts and you forgot to check one small detail. This is my job.' She stabbed at the printouts. 'I am a professional photographer. I dealt with computer photography almost every day of my working life. So I know without even bothering to enlarge the bedroom scene that the folds of the sheet don't quite follow a natural line.

The slight shrug of Diantha's shoulders and indifferent expression surprised Isobel because she should have been feeling the pinch of her own culpability by now. But she just smiled. 'You are such a fool, Isobel,' she told her. 'I have always known what you do for a living, and these photographs were always meant to be exposed as fakes. Indeed it is essential that I did so to allay a scandal. I merely intended to expose them myself for what they are, then suggest that you probably did these yourself as a way of increasing your power in a divorce settlement. For who else is better qualified?'

She believes she has everyone tied up in knots, Isobel realised in gaping incredulity. She is so supremely confident of her own powers of manipulation that she has stopped seeing the wood for the trees!

'There is only one small problem with your plan, Diantha,' Isobel said narrowly. 'These photographs may be fakes, but I have no reason to want a divorce.'

'But does he want you or is Leandros merely protecting his business interests?'

'Oh, yes, I want her,' a smooth, deep voice replied.

The two women glanced up, saw Leandros standing there and looking as if he had been for quite a long time.

'Every minute of every waking moment,' he added smoothly. 'Every minute of every moment I spend lost in my dreams. You have a serious problem with your dreams, Diantha,' he told her sombrely, then without waiting for a reply he looked at Isobel. 'Shall we go?'

She didn't even hesitate, walking towards this man who was her life, with her eyes loving him and his loving her by return.

But Diantha was not about to give up so easily. 'Just because these photographs are not real, it does not mean we did not sleep together,' she threaded in stealthily. 'Tell her, Leandros, how we spent the nights upon your yacht. Tell her how your mama thinks she is a tart and your sister Chloe despises every breath that she takes. Tell her,' she persisted, 'how your whole family knew she was having an affair with some man while she was here last, and how you tried to discover who he was and even believed the child she was carrying belonged to this other lover!'

Isobel's feet came to a shuddering standstill. Her eyes clouded as she searched his. She was looking for sorrow, for a weary shake of the head to deny what Diantha was saying! For goodness' sake, she begged him; give me anything to say that she's still manipulating me here!

But he'd gone as pale as she'd ever seen him. His fingers trembled as he lifted them up to run through his hair. Most damning of all, he lowered his eyes from her. 'Come on,' he said huskily. 'Let's get out of here.'

Someone else was standing just behind him, and as Leandros moved Isobel saw Chloe looking white-faced. 'Diantha, stop this,' Chloe pleaded unsteadily. 'I don't understand why you—'

'You don't understand.' Diantha turned on her scathingly. 'What has it got to do with you? Your brothers used me and I will not be used!'

Brothers? Each one of them looked at her when she said this. She was no longer calm and collected, Isobel noticed. The veils of control had been ripped away and suddenly Diantha was showing her true cold and bitter self.

'All my life I had to watch you, Chloe, being worshipped by your family of men. You have no idea what it is like to be unloved and rejected by anyone. My father rejected me because I was not a desired son. Your brother rejected me because I was not what he wanted any more.'

'Diantha, I never—'

'Not you,' she flashed at Leandros. 'Nikos! Nikos rejected me four years ago! He said we were too young to know what love was and he did not even want to know! But I knew love. I waited and waited in Washington for him to come for me. But he didn't,' she said bitterly. 'You came instead, offering me those pleasant messages from home and not one from Nikos! So I came back here to Athens to make him love me! But when I arrived he was planning to marry Carlotta. I was out in the cold and there you were, Leandros, hiding in Spain with your broken heart! Well, why should we not mend together? You were thinking about it, I know you were. You can lie to her all you like, but I know that it was for me that you told Uncle Takis to begin divorce proceedings with her!'

His eyes narrowed. 'So Takis has been talking out of line,' he murmured silkily.

'No!' she denied that. 'I have discussed this with no one.'

'Then how did you know there was no pre-nuptial agreement?' Isobel inserted sharply.

Diantha floundered, her mouth hovering on lies she could not find.

'I think this has gone far enough,' yet another voice intruded. It was Diantha's father. 'You have managed to stop the photographs being printed in the newspaper, Leandros?' he enquired. At Leandros's grim nod, he nodded also. 'Then please leave my house and take your family with you.'

Mr Christophoros had clearly decided that his daughter had hurt enough people for one day.

The journey away was completed in near silence. Chloe sat sharing the passenger seat in Leandros's Ferrari with Isobel, her face drawn with shock and dismay. Leandros took his sister home first, pulling up outside a house that was three times the size of his own. As she climbed out of the car, she turned back to Isobel.

'I'm sorry,' she whispered urgently. 'I never meant—'

'Later, Chloe,' her brother interrupted. 'We will all talk later but now Isobel and I have to go.'

'But most of this is my fault!' she cried out painfully. 'I encouraged her to believe that she was meant for one of my brothers—'

'Childhood stuff,' Leandros said dismissively.

'I let her know how much I disliked Isobel!'

Isobel's chin went down on her chest. Chloe released a choking sob. 'I confided everything to her and she took it all away and plotted with it. I can't tell you how bad that makes me feel.'

Isobel could see it all. The two girls sighing over Leandros's broken heart—as Diantha had called it. The two of them wishing that Isobel had never been born.

'But I never knew a thing about her and Nikos,' Chloe inserted in stifled disbelief.

'It was nothing,' her brother declared. 'They dated a couple of times while you were away at college, but Nikos was made wary by her tendency towards possessiveness. He told her so and she took it badly. He was relieved when her family went to live in Washington—and I would prefer you not to mention this to him, Chloe,' he then warned very seriously. 'He will not appreciate the reminder at this time.'

He was talking about Nikos's coming marriage. Chloe nodded then swallowed and tentatively touched Isobel's arm. 'Please,' she murmured, 'can you and I make a fresh start?'

A fresh start, Isobel repeated inwardly, and her eyes glazed over. Everyone wanted to make fresh starts, but how many more ugly skeletons were going to creep out of the dark cupboard before she felt safe enough to trust any one of them?

She lifted her face though, and smiled for Chloe. 'Of

course,' she agreed. But the way her voice shook had Leandros slamming the car into gear and gunning the engine. His sister stepped back, her face pale and anxious. Isobel barely managed to get the car door shut before he was speeding away with a hissing spin of gravel-flecked tyres.

'What's the matter with you?' she lashed out in reaction.

'If you are going to cry, then you will do it where I can damn well get at you,' he thrust back roughly.

'I am not going to cry.'

'Tell that to someone who cannot see beyond the tough outer layer.' He lanced her a look that almost seared off her skin. 'I did not sleep with her—*ever*!' he rasped, turned his eyes back to the road and rammed the car through its gears with a hand that resembled a white-knuckled fist. 'I *liked* her! But she has poison in her soul and now I can feel it poisoning me.' His voice suddenly turned hoarse. 'Did I give her reason to believe what she does about me? Did I offer encouragement without realising it?'

His hand left the wheel to run taut fingers through his hair. It was instinctive for Isobel to reach across and grab the wheel.

'You don't need to do that,' he gritted. 'I am not about to drive us into a wall.'

'Then stop acting like it.'

The car stopped with a screech of brakes. Isobel had not put on her seat belt because Chloe had been sharing her seat and the momentum took her head dangerously close to the windscreen before an arm shot out and halted the imminent clash with a fierce clenching of male muscle.

Emotions were flying about in all directions. Stress—distress! Anger—frustration. He threw open his door, climbed out and walked away a few long strides, leaving

Isobel sitting there in a state of blank bewilderment as to what it was that was the matter with him.

It was her place to be this upset, surely? She had been the one who'd had to place her trust on the line ever since she came back here! She got out of the car, turned and gave the beautiful, glossy red door a very expressive slam. He spun on his heel. She glared at him across the glossy red bonnet. They were within sight of their own driveway but neither seemed to care.

'Just who the hell do you think you are, Leandros?' she spat at him furiously. She was still responding to the shock of almost having her head smacked up against the windscreen; her insides were crawling with all kinds of throbs and flurries. He was pale—*she* was pale! The sun was beating down upon them and if she could have she would have reached up and grabbed it then thrown it at his bloody selfish head! 'What do you think her poison is doing to me? You want a divorce then you don't want a divorce. Rumour has it that you have your next wife already picked out and waiting in the wings. Pre-nuptial agreements are suddenly the all-important topic on everyone's lips! And I am expected to trust your word! Then I am expected to trust your word again when those photographs turn up. I even face the bitch with her so-called lies!'

'They are lies, you know that—'

'All I know for certain at this precise moment is that you have been working me like a puppet on a string!' she tossed at him furiously. 'I've been insulted in your boardroom—*stalked* around Athens—which appears is not the first time! I've been seduced at every available opportunity, teased over family heirlooms, paraded out in front of Athens' finest like a trophy that was not much of a prize!'

He laughed, but it was thick and tense. She almost climbed over the car bonnet to get her claws into him! 'Then I am forced to stare at those wr-wretched ph-photographs.' Her throat began to work; grimly she swallowed the threatening tears. 'Do you think because I could prove them to be fakes that they lost the power to hurt?'

'No.' He took a step towards the bonnet.

'I haven't finished!' she thrust at him thickly, and the glinting green bolts coming from her eyes pinned him still. '*I* faced the poison—while you went chasing off to the wrong place!' she declared hotly. 'I listened to her say all of those things about you and *still* believed in you. My God,' she choked. 'Why was that, do you think, when we only have to look back three years to see that we were heading right down the same road again?'

'It is not the same!' he blasted at her.

'It has the same nasty taste!' she cried. 'Your mother is prepared to *try* and like me for your sake and now your sister is prepared to do the same. Do I care if they like me?' Yes, I do, she thought painfully. 'No, I don't,' she said out loud. 'I don't think I care for you any more,' she whispered unsteadily.

'You don't mean that—'

She flicked his tight features a glance and wished to hell that she did mean it. 'Tell me about the pre-nuptial thing,' she challenged. 'Then go on to explain about this other man I am supposed to have fathered my child to. And then,' she continued when he opened his mouth to answer, 'explain to me why I have just had to listen to you bemoaning the poison that wretched woman has fed into you!'

Silence reigned. He looked totally stunned by the final question. A silver Mercedes came down the road. It stopped beside Isobel. 'Is something wrong?' a voice said. 'Can we be of assistance?'

Isobel turned to stare at Theron Herakleides. Beside him in the passenger seat, her mother was bending over to peer out curiously. 'Yes,' she said. 'You can give me a lift.' With that, she climbed into the back of the Mercedes.

'What about Leand—?'

'Just drive,' she snapped. Theron looked at her in blank astonishment. He had probably never been spoken to like this before in his life! Then she put a trembling hand up to cover her equally tremulous mouth. 'I'm sorry,' she apologised, and tears began to burn her eyes.

'Drive, Theron,' her mother murmured quietly. Without another word, Theron did as he was told, his glance shifting to his rear-view mirror, where he saw his nephew left standing by his car looking like a man who had just been hit by a car.

Watching his uncle Theron drive away with Isobel, Leandros was feeling as if he had been hit—by an absolute hellion with a torrent that poured from her mouth.

How had she done it? How had she managed to leave him standing here, feeling like the most selfish bastard alive on this planet?

Because you are, a voice in his head told him. Because there was not a word she'd said that did not ring true.

Ah. He spun around to stare blankly at his native city spread out beneath him and shimmering in a late-morning haze, and instead saw a jigsaw of words come to dance in front of his eyes. Words like, insulted, stalked, seduced—trophy. He uttered the same tense, half-amused laugh then wasn't laughing at all because she believed it to be the truth.

Just as she believed that he suspected their baby could have belonged to another man. His heart came to a stop, thudding as it landed at the base of his stomach as he joined that new belief with her old belief that he was glad when she miscarried. And what had he done? He'd sat beside her in his car and voiced concerns about his behaviour towards Diantha.

Was he mad? He turned around. Did she accuse him of possessing the sensitivity of a flea? Because if she did not then she should have done. Where the hell had his head been? he asked himself furiously.

What was he doing standing here when there was every chance she was packing to leave him right now?

Damn, he cursed, and climbed into his car. The engine fired; he pushed it in gear. If her suitcase was out then he was in deep trouble, he accepted as he covered the fifty yards to his driveway at breakneck speed.

Theron's car was already parked outside the front door and empty of its passengers. Striding into the house, he didn't think twice about where to look for her and took the stairs three at a time, arriving outside their bedroom before he paused then diverted to the room next door.

Thrusting the door open, he stepped inside. His instincts had not let him down. She was standing by the window, facing into the room with her arms folded.

Waiting for him, he noted with grim satisfaction, and closed the door. 'I did not believe you had been unfaithful to me,' he stated as he strode forward. 'The only marriage contract that you and I will ever have will have to be written in my blood on my deathbed since I have no intention of letting you go before I die. I do not think of you as a trophy, a puppet or a thing of mockery. And I don't *stalk* you, I *follow* you like some bloody faithful pet dog who does not want to be anywhere else but where you are.'

He came to a stop in front of her. Her eyes were dark, her mouth small and her hair was stuck in a pony-tail. She was wearing combat trousers and a tough-lady vest top but there were tears sliding down both smooth cheeks.

'If I loved you any more than I do already they would have to put me away because I would be dangerous,' he continued huskily. 'And if I sounded bloody insensitive back there then that is because I was hurt by those photographs too.'

She stifled a small sob. He refused to reach for her. He would answer all charges and *then* he would touch.

'Diantha has been a part of my family since she and Chloe were giggling schoolgirls. I believed Nikos had hurt her four years ago, I thought he had deliberately set out to turn her head and when she became serious left her flat. I even felt sorry for her so I visited whenever I was in Washington. But Nikos now tells me that he recognised her need to manipulate even then. I was wrong about her and now I am sorry—and don't think those tears are going to save you,' he added, 'because they are not.'

'Save me from what?'

'Retribution,' he answered. 'For daring to believe I could question the parentage of our child.'

'Your face—'

'My face was pained, I know,' he admitted. 'There is only one person who could have put such a filthy idea in her head and that is Takis. And how do I know that? Because he once dared to suggest such a thing to me.'

'Takis…?' Her eyelashes fluttered, tear-tipped and sparkling.

He rasped out a sigh that fell between anger and hurt. 'I was miserable, you were miserable,' he reminded her. 'We were living within a vacuum where we did not communicate. Takis was the closest thing I had to a father back then. He asked about our marriage, and when I stupidly said in a weak moment that I was worried about you because you were forever going missing he suggested that maybe I should find out where you go.'

He clamped his mouth shut over the rest of that conversation. What it contained did not matter here. What did was that his most trusted friend and employer had been passing on confidential information. 'Now I find he has been disclosing confidential information about pre-nuptial contracts and the lack of.'

'Did he set up the photographer too?'

He sighed and shook his head. 'I am hoping he did not. I am hoping that the photographs were all Diantha's idea. Has it occurred to you that she had taken those things before she knew that you and I would get back together? Which means she always planned to use them whether or not you were still on the scene. A safeguard,' he called it. 'In case I did not come through with the marriage proposal. How do you think it makes me feel to know I was open to such manipulation?'

'An idiot, I guess.' She offered him a shrug that said she believed he deserved it. Insolence did not begin to cover the expression on her beautiful face.

His eyes narrowed. Challenge was suddenly back in the air. Then without warning she issued a thick sob then fell into his arms—because she belonged there.

'I've had a h-horrible day,' she sobbed against him.

'I can change that,' he promised, picked her up and took her to the bed. They could make love—why not? It was the most effective cleanser of poison that he knew of.

Afterwards they went downstairs to find their home overrun by people who wanted to make amends for all the ugliness. His mother was there, his sister, Chloe, even Nikos had come with Carlotta pinned possessively to his side. Silvia and Theron were looking shell-shocked because someone had run the whole sequence of events by them.

No Takis Konstantindou though, he noticed, and felt a short wave of anger-cum-regret flood his mind. Takis was out, and he probably knew it by now. Diantha's father would have seen to it. He was a man of honour despite what his daughter was.

Eve arrived with Ethan Hayes, carrying a crate of champagne. 'To welcome Isobel back into the fold,' Eve announced, but they all knew that she'd heard about today's events too.

'You don't need jungle drums up here,' Isobel whispered to Leandros. 'The rumours get round on a current of air!'

But her cheeks were flushed and she was happy. The doorbell sounded and two minutes later another visitor stepped onto the sunny terrace. 'My God, I don't believe it,' Leandros gasped in warm surprise—while everyone else was thrown into silence by the sight of the dauntingly aloof Felipe Vazquez, while he appeared taken aback by so many curious faces. 'When did you get into town?'

'My apologies for the intrusion,' he murmured stiffly.

'No intrusion at all,' Leandros assured and took him to meet his beautiful wife, who stared up at his friend as if what she was seeing lit a vision in her head.

Leandros grinned as he watched it happen. 'No,' he bent to murmur close to her ear. 'Felipe is Spanish, not Venezuelan.'

'Oh,' she pouted up at him. 'What a terrible shame.'

The afternoon took on a festive quality. By the time everyone drifted away again, Isobel was looking just a little bewildered. 'We seem to have become very popular all of a sudden,' she said.

'Too popular,' he answered. 'After Nikos's wedding you

and I are flying to the Caribbean to gatecrash his honeymoon,' he said decisively.

'But we can't do that!' Isobel protested.

'Why not?' he countered. 'He intends to cruise on my yacht. I intend that we stay so stationary that it will be an effort to move from the bed to the terrace. But for now,' he began to stalk her, 'you owe me something I am about to collect.'

'Owe you what?' she demanded.

'Humble pie?' he softly reminded her.

Modern Romance™
...seduction and
passion guaranteed

Tender Romance™
...love affairs that
last a lifetime

Sensual Romance™
...sassy, sexy and
seductive

Blaze Romance™
...the temperature's
rising

Medical Romance™
...medical drama on
the pulse

Historical Romance™
...rich, vivid and
passionate

27 new titles every month.

*With all kinds of Romance for
every kind of mood...*

Don't miss *Book Seven* of this BRAND-NEW 12 book collection 'Bachelor Auction'.

Who says money can't buy love?

On sale 7th March

FREE!

2 Books
and a surprise gift!

We would like to take this opportunity to thank you for reading this Mills & Boon® book by offering you the chance to take TWO more specially selected titles from the Modern Romance™ series absolutely FREE! We're also making this offer to introduce you to the benefits of the Reader Service™—

- ★ FREE home delivery
- ★ FREE gifts and competitions
- ★ FREE monthly Newsletter
- ★ Books available before they're in the shops
- ★ Exclusive Reader Service discount

Accepting these FREE books and gift places you under no obligation to buy; you may cancel at any time, even after receiving your free shipment. Simply complete your details below and return the entire page to the address below. **You don't even need a stamp!**

YES! Please send me 2 free Modern Romance books and a surprise gift. I understand that unless you hear from me, I will receive 4 superb new titles every month for just £2.55 each, postage and packing free. I am under no obligation to purchase any books and may cancel my subscription at any time. The free books and gift will be mine to keep in any case.

P3ZEB

Ms/Mrs/Miss/Mr ....Initials..............................
BLOCK CAPITALS PLEASE

Surname..

Address..

....

....Postcode ....

Send this whole page to:
UK: The Reader Service, FREEPOST CN81, Croydon, CR9 3WZ
EIRE: The Reader Service, PO Box 4546, Kilcock, County Kildare (stamp required)

Offer not valid to current Reader Service subscribers to this series. We reserve the right to refuse an application and applicants must be aged 18 years or over. Only one application per household. Terms and prices subject to change without notice. Offer expires 30th May 2003. As a result of this application, you may receive offers from Harlequin Mills & Boon and other carefully selected companies. If you would prefer not to share in this opportunity please write to The Data Manager at the address above.

Mills & Boon® is a registered trademark owned by Harlequin Mills & Boon Limited.
Modern Romance™ is being used as a trademark.